The Empire o

Book Three of the Chronicles of

the Second Interstellar Empire of

Mankind

By

Robert I. Katz

The Empire of Dust:

Book Three of the Chronicles of the Second

Interstellar Empire of Mankind

Also by Robert I. Katz

Edward Maret: A Novel of the Future

The Cannibal's Feast

The Kurtz and Barent Mystery Series:
Surgical Risk
The Anatomy Lesson
Seizure
The Chairmen

The Chronicles of the Second Interstellar Empire of
Mankind:
The Game Players of Meridien
The City of Ashes
The Empire of Dust

Prologue

He groaned as the cold slowly seeped into his awareness. Dimly, he felt that he might have shivered but he wasn't certain of this. He was numb. Am I alive? He thought that he must be. I think, therefore…how did that go? Something. The thought hung there in the back of his brain, elusive. Slowly, he wriggled his fingers, then his toes. He tried to blink his eyes but the darkness was absolute. Maybe he succeeded. He couldn't tell. Fingers and toes then. He wriggled them again then clenched his fists. *If I have hands then I must have arms, and legs*. That was a comforting thought. Arms and legs were good, at least a start. He tried to cry out but something liquid and harsh filled his mouth.

Wait, a voice seemed to say. Everything will be explained. Give it time. Was this his own thought or did it come from somewhere outside? Something that might have been amusement filled his mind. He had nowhere to go and nothing but time.

For a time then, he slept.

Chapter 1

The planet was dusty, almost barren, but there was life. It clustered around the oases and on the coasts, people struggling to make a living. Their database listed the world as Baldur-3, the third world in the Baldur system. The local web was unshielded and easy to access. The city below them was called Norwich.

"What do you think?" Michael Glover asked.

"We need fuel," Romulus said. "They have fuel."

Deuterium for the fusion generators. They had jumped far and this was the first human settled world they had come across in over a month that was more than a series of ruins. "I don't know," Michael said. "They're not exactly high tech."

"High enough. The world is clean and orderly. There are three universities on the Western continent and another five on the Eastern. They're not barbarians. They'll have what we need."

Michael shrugged. "Better than nothing."

The ship's sensors had revealed a landing field on a large island off the coast of the Eastern continent. He instructed the AI to approach. They were hailed when still fifty kilometers up. "Unknown ship. State your business and world of origin."

"This is the starship *London*," Michael said. "Out of Beta Ionis-4." It was nonsense, of course. Beta Ionis was a rocky, frozen system with a population of sentient, low temperature aliens that had never developed interstellar travel. Humanity had been trading with them for thousands of years.

The voice seemed to hesitate. "We have no record of human habitation in the Beta-Ionis system."

"We maintain a habitat in the asteroid belt." This was true, or it was true in the days of the Empire. Regardless, it was not a statement that could be disproven from half a galaxy away.

"Please state your business."

"The *London* is a merchant vessel. I have a cargo to sell and I wish to purchase deuterium."

"The names of your crew?"

"There is only myself. My name is Michael Glover."

After a moment, the voice said. "You may land. Please follow the beacon to slip number eight."

Twenty minutes later, the *London* settled into the designated location. Up close, the port was busier than Michael had expected. Cargo carriers rolled across the dusty tarmac. Three other slips were occupied, all with ships somewhat smaller than their own. "I think you should stay aboard," Michael said. "Actually, you should stay hidden."

Romulus looked nothing like *Homo Sapiens*. His matte black composite structure possessed arms, legs and a head only as a concession to human sensibilities. Romulus nodded. Without a word, he pressed a panel in the wall of the main cabin. The panel slid open. The robot entered and the panel slid seamlessly closed.

Five minutes later, the port inspectors arrived, one small, young and female, the other male, of indeterminate age, with a harried expression on his face. Michael pressed a button. A metal ramp unfolded and the main airlock opened. The inspectors entered, glancing curiously around the cabin. "Captain Glover?" The male inspector held out a hand. Michael took it. "I'm Chief Inspector Mark Conway. This is Assistant Inspector Natalie Levin. Welcome to Baldur."

Natalie Levin frowned. "You're really the only one aboard? I've heard of fully automated ships. I've never seen one."

Michael smiled. "We're proud of it. It's a copy of an ancient First Empire design."

"Well, we'll need to inspect your cargo."

"Feel free."

The cargo had been carefully chosen. Little of it was high tech, mainly inexpensive but no longer up-to-date pre-fab matrices and solid state transistors that could be adapted to a variety of computer platforms, spices from five different worlds that had been stored in liquid nitrogen for over two thousand years, a lockbox of uncut jewels, most of them unique to their own worlds of origin, another lockbox containing small ingots of gold and another of platinum, and pallets of spider silk from the jungles of Rigel.

Natalie Levin pursed her lips when she saw the manifest and frowned at Michael. "You can't trade the spices here unless you get authorization from the medical authorities declaring them safe for human consumption. Also, the matrices might contain viruses that our own computers aren't equipped to handle. You're not allowed to sell them or let them connect to the local web. The rest of it is approved." She tore a sheet of paper off a clipboard. "Post this in your cargo bay where prospective buyers can see it. Good luck."

"An interesting cargo," Conway said. "You've travelled widely."

"It's what I do," Michael said. "Buy low and sell high." It was a plausible statement but not exactly the truth. It could easily become the truth, however. He had to do something to occupy his time and whatever that something ultimately turned out to be, an itinerant merchant captain made an excellent cover.

"Your papers are in order," Conway said. "I suggest that you head over to the merchant's guild. They'll put you in touch with potential buyers." He glanced at a comp on his wrist. "Too late tonight, though. They open first thing in the morning."

"Thank you," Michael said. "I'll do that. Meanwhile, what is there to do at night in your fair city?" Calling it a city was definitely a stretch but it never hurt to be polite.

Natalie Levin snorted. "Not much," she said.

Conway smiled at her. "We have some excellent restaurants, a zoo and a museum. There are a number of local sports teams but none of them are playing this evening. Two small theaters offer live entertainment. One of them is playing *Twelfth Night*, the 5714 translation. Also, the local web carries numerous channels. If you want to get off your ship, there are three reasonable hotels in the center of town." He shrugged. "Good luck."

They shook hands again, Michael thanked them both and waited until they had gone and the airlock closed behind them before saying, "What do you think?"

Romulus' voice issued from a speaker grid near the ceiling. "Everything seems in order. I'm not expecting trouble."

"No," Michael said. "It all seems very civilized."

Chapter 2

When he had awakened for the second time, he found that he was stronger. He opened his eyes and could see light. He was lying on a soft mattress on a narrow bed and covered by a white sheet. A monitor hanging near the ceiling displayed his temperature, a picture of his beating heart with digital readout of the blood flow through each coronary artery, electrocardiogram with heart rate, and oxygen saturation. The values were all normal. He frowned at the heart rate. *Normal*, after all, is relative. Statistically, 'normal' means average. He was supposed to be better than normal. A conditioned athlete should have a heart rate lower than the average. He would have to work on that when he got out of here. No doubt, he would be required to do so. Grimly, he thought that he would not have been awakened without a reason.

But where was here? Many, many years ago, he had chosen to serve the Empire and after that initial choice, the choices given him had been few. He sighed, held up his right hand in front of his face and flexed the fist. It looked like his hand, the hand that he remembered. It looked…normal. He smiled and drifted back to sleep.

When he awoke for a third time, he felt almost himself. He noted the slow drip of the IV line, feeding a milky white fluid into a vein. Daylight shone in through the window. "Hello?" he said.

There was no answer and he considered swinging his legs over the side of the bed. Sooner or later, he would have to get up, if only to empty his bladder. Might as well be now. A ping came from the monitor. "Please state your name."

The request was routine. He had known it would be coming. One out of ten thousand, for reasons not perfectly understood, did not survive the freezing process. Twice that number awoke with at least minimal brain damage, most commonly transient amnesia. "Michael Glover," he said.

"Your date of birth?"

"April 17, 3912, Imperial calendar."

"Excellent," the voice said. "Please wait."

For what? He smiled to himself. He was well acquainted with bureaucracy. Hurry up and wait was standard operating procedure in all bureaucratic organizations, but he didn't have to wait long. The door opened and a thin, humanoid robot entered the room. The robot was constructed of a black composite material. It had legs, arms and a head. Aside from a speaker grill and two optic sensors about where a mouth and eyes would be on a human, the head was otherwise featureless. Michael noted the sensor grid displayed on its abdomen. The robot walked up to the side of the bed and stopped. "How are you feeling?" it asked.

"A little weak, otherwise fine."

The robot cocked its head. "That is to be expected. Please refer to me as Romulus." The robot scanned the monitor screen, nodded in an absurd parody of a human gesture, deftly removed the IV line and covered the puncture with a small bandage, all of which Michael tolerated without comment. The robot stepped back from the bed and said, "I am to explain your mission."

Michael smiled. No sense in waiting. "Please do."

"Not here," the robot said. "Follow me." It turned and walked out the door.

Michael scrambled out of bed. He was naked. The simulated display in the upper corner of his visual field gave him the ambient temperature and atmospheric composition: exactly twenty degrees, not quite seventy-nine percent nitrogen, twenty-one percent oxygen, a scattering of trace gasses, perfectly safe and comfortable. The robot paused in the doorway, turned its head and waited until Michael felt steady on his feet, then resumed walking. Michael followed.

Chapter 3

The port was situated at the edge of the city, bounded by woods on two sides, with a grassy plain to the west that ended at an isthmus separating the island from the mainland, and a distant glow of city lights to the east. Michael had been cooped up in the ship for almost a month. He was eager to sample the fresh air of a new world and he decided to walk into town. The spiral arm of the milky way shone brightly overhead. The breeze was cool, the air fresh and filled with the scents of springtime flowers. After a half an hour, he came to the first row of small houses, then another and soon after, a row of two and three story office buildings, mostly empty now. He passed a few pedestrians, then more and soon he came to a central square that was almost crowded, lined with shops and restaurants.

There were a lot of families strolling about, three and four generations together. They seemed to marry young here and have a lot of kids. More than half carried weapons, some knives in belt sheaths, a few holstered pistols. He wandered into a clothing shop. The goods were all local. Spider silk might fetch a good price, he thought. He nodded to the proprietor and walked back out to the street.

A lit sign across the square said "Norwich Tavern." He was hungry and taverns were always good places to pick up gossip, though the word 'tavern' might have a different meaning on this world than on others; but he liked the place immediately. The floor was wood, with dark paneling on the walls, solid wooden booths and tables, comfortable looking chairs and a long wooden bar covering one whole side of the room. Most of the booths and about half the tables were occupied. A waitress, middle aged, slim, brunette and pretty greeted him at the door. "You can sit anywhere," she said. "Someone will be right with you."

He took a booth near the center of the row that gave him a good view of the room and picked up the menu. The general headings were obvious but some of the meats were obscure. What was a lapwing? The waitress who had greeted him walked up a few minutes later with a table setting and a glass of water. "Anything to drink?"

"Draft beer," he said. "Whatever's good."

"Well, that's a matter of opinion, but the Hofheiser Golden is probably our biggest seller."

"I'll have that," he said, and ordered a sandwich of something that the menu described as, 'slow roasted barbecued quagga on wheat bread.' It came with soup, a salad of mixed greens and dessert. He had his doubts about the rest of it but was looking forward to dessert.

The waitress smiled. "Be right back."

At its most sensitive level, and particularly in a crowd, Michael's augmented hearing could be overwhelming, even painful. He normally adjusted it to human baseline. He sub-vocalized a code and the tiny server beneath his sagittal sinus increased the auditory input so that even whispers from the furthest corner of the room could be picked up. A table near the back held five men from a starship crew but their conversation told Michael nothing he didn't already know. They were heading out in the morning, having sold their cargo for a decent price and re-invested the proceeds in ironwood, a local product popular on several nearby worlds. Pirate activity had been reported but none in this sector. The Empire patrols had not reached this far out yet but presumably would in a few more years. The Empire was expanding. The crew was not sure how they felt about this. Neither was Michael.

Michael's beer arrived. He sipped it, nodded in approval. Cold, with a lot of hops. The food arrived a minute later, first the soup, which wasn't bad, then the salad, nondescript but inoffensive. The sandwich was excellent, the meat tender and smoky.

In the back corner, two men were about to arm wrestle. One was big and burly with a shaved, bald head, pale white skin, enormous shoulders and a bushy beard. The other had a lined, sunburnt face and clothes that did not appear to have been recently washed. A small crowd was gathered around the table.

"Two credits on Rangel," one of them said.

A second one looked at the competitors and narrowed his eyes. "I'll take that bet. Curly will destroy him."

Curly, presumably the bald guy, looked up and grinned. The two competitors locked hands and one of the spectators, who seemed to be the designated referee, said, "Go."

Curly did not seem to be straining and the easy smile never left his face. The back of Rangel's hand slammed down on the table. Rangel shook his head. "Shit," he said, and rose to his feet.

"Anybody else?" Curly said.

Michael toyed with the idea of trying his luck but decided against it. He didn't need the money and he didn't want any trouble. He finished the sandwich and waited for dessert. One of the spacers rose to his feet and ambled to the back of the room. "How about me?" he said.

Curly frowned. "Where you from?"

The spacer grinned. "Scorpius Lambda."

"Scorpius Lambda is high gravity," Curly said.

The spacer nodded. "That's right."

Curly looked him up and down. "You have any other mods or implants? All natural?"

"Just me," the spacer said.

The spacer's comrades had all walked over and joined the crowd around the table. They were grinning. Michael shook his head. Curly frowned, then shrugged his massive shoulders. "Why not?" he said.

The spacer took the seat opposite Curly. He gave the crowd a speculative look. "Let's give the boys a little time to place their bets."

The crowd seemed interested in the bout but most were reluctant to put money on the outcome. Michael smiled to himself and rose to his feet. Something about the spacer annoyed him. "Fifty credits on Curly," he said.

One of the spacer's friends grinned. "You sure about that?"

"Fifty credits."

Curly looked pained but didn't say anything. The spacer gave Michael a wolfish smile. "Such easy money," he said.

"Anybody else?" the referee asked. "No?" He gave the crowd a second to think it over, then said, "Begin."

Tendons like small, steel cables bunched up on the spacer's forearm. For a moment, Curly's arm quivered, then firmed. Slowly,

Curly smiled. The spacer's face grew red, then his arm slammed down. "You lose," Curly said.

Michael turned to the spacer who had taken his bet. "Pay up."

The spacer's lips thinned and his breathing came faster. For a moment, Michael thought he might actually try to start something, then the guy shrugged, reached into his belt pack and pulled out a roll of the local currency. He counted out fifty credits and handed it over, not saying a word.

"Thanks," Michael said. He grinned. "Time for dessert."

Chapter 4

They had walked down an empty corridor, then another. It was quiet, the only sound the soft hum of blowers feeding breathable air into the installation. They passed nobody else. Finally, they walked through a door and into a circular room that his sensors told him was 10.2 meters in diameter. A walkway with a railing ran around a central holo tank with a circular console set in the floor underneath it. Inside the tank, rotating below the ceiling, a blue and green planet floated, surrounded by three small moons.

Romulus walked up to the tank, passed his hand over a series of glowing disks in the console. The globe stopped its rotation. A small yellow light appeared on a large body of land, close to an ocean. "This is a holograph of the world that we are on, called Arnett, named for William Arnett, who led the first expedition. It's a medium sized, Earth like planet near the edge of the Empire, or what used to be the Empire."

Michael frowned and looked at the robot. "How long?" he asked.

Romulus seemed to hesitate. "As you know, the Empire was invaded by an alien race, called the Hirrill. The Hirrill are now extinct, but the war lasted for over a century and in the chaos that followed, a renegade general named Thomas Montgomery attempted a political takeover. In the end, the Empire suffered a complete socio-economic collapse. The Empire ceased to exist and interstellar travel came to an almost complete halt. Humanity died out on perhaps twenty percent of the worlds that they had formerly inhabited. Others evolved in ways that we would consider anomalous, even strange. Perhaps five hundred years ago, Reliance, one of the earliest of the human settled worlds, returned to space and began to gather the remnants of the former Empire together. There is a new Empire, not as technologically advanced as the First Empire, not as large, but it is real. It is growing and expanding."

Michael sighed. Not good. Not good at all. "I asked you how long."

"Two thousand years. Thomas Montgomery was assassinated, along with his staff. Afterwards, there was civil war. You were forgotten, along with almost everything else."

All gone, he thought. All of it. Everything I ever was, everyone I ever knew. He felt numb. He shook his head and drew a deep breath. "Who else is here?"

"Nobody. You are the only human on this base. You are, in fact, the only human being on this world."

"Why now? Why was I awakened?"

"Arnett has an eccentric orbit around its sun, with fifty years of summer followed by almost five hundred years of freezing winter. It was one of the last settled worlds of the Empire and the small population of humanity died off or emigrated well over a thousand years ago. It was never the most pleasant place for human beings to live. There is nothing left beyond this base. Recently, a sun went supernova, only twenty-three light years away. This world is about to be scoured clean by radiation. If you are still here when the radiation blast hits Arnett, you will die."

"If?" Michael said. "Do I have a choice?"

"We have three ships in storage. We intend for you to leave this world."

He shook his head and sighed again. It was hard to get his brain to function. Not what he had been expecting, not at all. If this robot could be believed, and he had no reason to doubt it, the Empire that he had served was gone, and with it all of his friends, his family, his home; but he was a soldier and soldiers learn to soldier on. He was alive and he was awake and apparently, arrangements had been made for him to keep on living. Better than the alternative, he supposed. He shook his head and tried to concentrate on the most immediate concerns. There would be plenty of time later to sit and consider all the implications of what Romulus had told him. "You mentioned a mission," he said.

"Yes, I did. More of a goal, really. I was created to serve the Empire. You were sworn to its service. The Empire as it was, all those years ago, is no more but the essence of the Empire still exists, its goals, at least, its rationale and reason for being. The Empire was created to extend order and human hegemony over all the known worlds. This is a struggle that shall never cease. Your mission is to go forth from this world and to assist the forces of mankind in whatever way seems best."

"Rather open ended," Michael said. Also, complete bullshit. Despite the robot's noble sounding rhetoric, the Empire apparently was gone. His chain of command no longer existed and robots were not authorized to issue orders to Empire personnel.

Romulus shrugged. "We do what we have to. We do what we can."

"Can't argue with that," Michael said.

Chapter 5

Dessert was a slice of yellow cake interspersed with layers of sweet creamy cheese, with a few unidentifiable berries on top. He enjoyed it. He was sipping from a cup of tea (no coffee on this world, alas), thinking about heading back to the ship when Curly sat down on the other side of the table. "Why did you bet on me?" he asked. Curly had an earnest look on his face.

"They were arrogant. They annoyed me."

"Fifty credits is a lot of money. I might have lost."

"I've been to Scorpius Lambda. They're built like rocks. The spacer has been away for too long. He probably doesn't even realize it himself but you can see it in the way he walks, in the size of his chest and his arms. He's still stronger than most but he's not as strong as he used to be."

Curly, on the other hand, was enormous. Michael would have bet that there were some high gravity genes somewhere in his ancestry.

Curly frowned, obviously considering Michael's statement. "Okay." He held his hand out for Michael to shake. "Thanks," he said, and returned to his friends in the back of the room.

Michael finished his tea and rose to his feet. He liked this place. It was pleasant and comfortable and reminded him of home. The beer was good, the food better than most. He actually toyed with the idea of staying, at least for awhile but it seemed, in the end, to be a boring little world. Pleasant, though. He sighed. Most likely, after tonight he would never see the place again.

It was late and the streets outside the tavern by now were almost deserted but the night was still warm and he enjoyed the stroll. Soon, he seemed to be alone and Michael smiled to himself because somebody, and he would have taken bets that he knew exactly who it had to be, was following him. Three of them...no, four, the last one trailing behind the others.

Men, he could deal with, unless they had guns...which they well might. Guns would change things. Michael had a gun of his own, strapped to his leg in an ankle holster but he would much prefer not to kill anybody tonight. It would cast a pall over what had been a pleasant evening.

The woods clustered tightly together along this section of road. He turned, took three steps to the side and vanished behind a tree. He heard running, then they were blundering in after him. Stupid. His augmented senses told him where they were with pinpoint accuracy, the navigational grid implanted in his retina giving him a visual guide to their positions that he did not actually need. He stepped out, grabbed the last one in line by the neck, pulled him into the brush and rammed him face first into a tree. One down. He searched him quickly, came up with a knife but no gun.

The remaining two were evidently not used to fighting in the woods and the dark. They should have thought of that before. Idiots. They blundered around like blind men. Michael laughed out loud. They heard him and they froze, suddenly realizing that they were no longer the hunters; they were the prey.

"It's time for you boys to leave," Michael said. "And take this other moron with you."

No answer. He could hear them moving through the woods, trying to flank him. He shook his head sadly. Well, he had given them fair warning. He put his back to a tree and waited.

The first one came in from the side, his knife held low. He wasn't exactly an amateur. He knew how to use a blade but he wasn't nearly fast enough. Michael turned very slightly and the knife missed his chest by a centimeter. He grabbed the wrist and squeezed. The knife dropped to the ground. Michael twisted and the spacer screamed as the lower portion of his radius snapped. Michael raised his knee, pulled down and the spacer's nose crunched. He went limp. Michael let him drop, pulled a collapsible baton from his pocket and extended it with a flick of his wrist.

The other one was a little smarter than his friend. He came in slower, wary and uncertain of what he faced.

Michael shook his head. "I suppose you think that I'm supposed to care about your stupid problems?" He sighed. "See, it's just not my job to keep you from betting money that you can't afford to lose."

The guy said nothing, which was smart of him. Concentrate on the fight. The fight is important. The fight is the only thing that's important. You can talk later, after the fight is over…if you're still alive.

So slow.

He lunged. Michael hit him in the hand with the baton. The spacer grunted. His knife dropped to the ground. "You're a fool," Michael observed. The spacer looked around wildly, for what reason, Michael couldn't fathom. Nobody was about to magically appear and save his stupid ass. Then the spacer turned and ran; definitely the smartest thing he'd done all night.

It was silent. The air still smelled fresh. The stars still shone. Michael breathed deeply and sighed. "Come on out," he said.

A large blur separated itself from the brush and stood up straight.

"What are you doing here?" Michael said.

"I thought you might need some help," Curly said.

Michael considered this. Curly shuffled his feet. "Thanks," Michael said.

"I guess you didn't," Curly said.

"No." Michael grinned. "I didn't, but thanks," he said again.

"Gonna leave those two here?"

"Might as well. They're not my problem. They'll wake up sooner or later, or their friends will come and get them."

Curly grunted.

"What's your story, Curly?"

"Not much to say. I got tired of farming. I got four brothers and two sisters. The folks got plenty of people to run the farm."

"So what do you want?"

"You need any crew? I'd like to go off-world, see what's out there."

Michael's first impulse was *hell, no*, but then, again... "You have any training?"

"Just on the web. I have machinist certification. I'm a pretty fair mechanic."

Not that it mattered. Truthfully, Michael didn't need any help in running the ship but you never did know when a few extra hands might be useful. "Anybody looking for you? The police, maybe?"

Curly looked offended. "Hell, no. My pa is twice my size. He would have tanned my hide."

"Twice your size, huh?"

Curly nodded. "One thing, though," he said.

Michael sighed. "Of course. Just one thing. One *more* thing."

"I've got a girlfriend, name's Rosanna. I don't go nowhere without her."

"Let me make sure I understand—you want me to hire you *and* your girlfriend?"

Curly nodded.

"And what extraordinary skills does this Rosanna bring to the party?"

"Huh?" Curly said.

"How is Rosanna supposed to earn her way?"

"She can cook."

"The ship has an auto-chef. Why would we need a cook?"

"Auto-chef?" Curly reared back in disbelief. "An auto-chef can't cook like Rosanna. She's an artist!"

"An artist," Michael said.

Curly nodded, then stood silent, waiting, his face resembling that of a beseeching, hopeful bear.

The ship was big enough to get lost in. He would barely have to see them if he didn't feel like it and if they turned out to be annoying, Curly and his girlfriend could be dropped off at the next civilized world with some experience spacing and a few credits that they wouldn't have done much to earn. Finally, Michael scratched the side of his head. "Alright, why don't you go and fetch this artist? Be at my ship by noon, tomorrow. If you're not there on time, we'll leave without you."

Curly's eyes lit up. "We'll be there! Thanks."

Michael sighed. "Don't mention it."

Chapter 6

There were more than two thousand worlds in the First Interstellar Empire of Mankind, all of them different but all of them much the same. Water worlds, jungle worlds, desert worlds. Low gravity worlds where modified humans with hollow bones and bat like wings flew through the air and perched on the branches of mutated redwoods, three hundred meters tall. Frozen worlds where humans with fur and a thick layer of subcutaneous fat lived cold, comfortable lives. People lived in space habitats floating in orbit and they lived on tiny asteroids far from the sun and they swam into watery homes at the bottom of deep, blue oceans, breathing through their gills. All of them swore allegiance to the Imperator. All paid taxes to the Imperial treasury. All of them sent their sons and daughters to serve when needed.

"What are you doing?" young Michael Glover asked.

"Nothing." His sister looked at him, her eyes wide and skittish. She brushed past him, went into her room, closed and locked the door. He stood there in the hallway, uncertain. After a moment, he thought that he heard muffled sobbing but it stopped after a few seconds. Maybe he imagined it.

A few seconds later, his stepfather walked down the hallway. He wore a robe, loosely belted at the waist. His face was red. He looked angry. He barely nodded to Michael as he walked past and into the room that he shared with Michael's mother. The door clicked closed.

Michael's sister, Diane, was fourteen, a pretty girl who had until recently been bubbly and vibrant. Lately, her mood had grown subdued. She smiled little and spent most of her time alone in her room.

Michael watched the next afternoon as she arrived home from school, trudging up the walkway, clutching her books to her chest, shoulders hunched. "What is he doing to you?" he said.

She gave a little gasp. "Michael," she said, "I didn't see you."

"What is he doing to you?" he repeated.

He thought for a moment that she would deny it but then she shrugged. "He grabs me when Mom isn't looking. He tries to kiss me."

"That's all?"

"So far."

"Why haven't you complained?"

She swallowed. "You know how Mom is."

Their mother had suffered from clinical depression after her first husband's death. She had been confined to a psychiatric ward for almost a month. Her current husband, Janek Pryor, was minor nobility and very rich. Frankly, nobody could quite understand it when the second son of Lord Pryor began paying attention to the widow of one of his retainers. Oh, Dianna Glover was pretty, even beautiful, but she was poor and no longer young. She had young daughters, however, two of them.

And one son.

"Has he touched Susan?"

Diane shook her head. "She's only nine."

"So?"

"That's disgusting," Diane said. She said it mildly. It may have been disgusting but it was obvious that Diane had been asking herself the same question. "No," she said. "I would have known."

"Small favors. Sooner or later, he'll try."

"He said that nobody would believe me."

"I see," Michael said, and he smiled.

Diane's face grew suddenly pale. "What are you going to do?" she said.

"Nothing," Michael said. "Nothing at all."

"So, young man..." The police inspector peered down at his wrist comp, then gave Michael a knowing smile. "Where were you at two-fifteen this afternoon?"

"Watching a holo in my room."

"By yourself?"

"Yes."

"Not much of an alibi, is it?"

Michael shrugged. The policeman's grin grew wider. "Terrible accident, though, isn't it?"

"Things happen," Michael said.

The inspector made a *tsk-tsk* sound between his teeth and tapped his pen idly on the desk. "Indeed they do. In this case, a bookshelf seems to have toppled over, apparently hitting Janek Pryor above the waist. He fell, struck his head on the edge of a table and snapped his neck. He died almost immediately."

Michael nodded. "So I understand."

"You don't look grief stricken."

Michael shrugged. "I feel bad for my mother."

"First your father, now this." The inspector looked genuinely regretful. "I would hate to add to your mother's burdens." The inspector leaned back in his chair, gave Michael a look of faint disapproval and shook his head. "Janek Pryor has extensive bruising on his face and the sides of his neck. His trachea has been crushed. The damage seems disproportional. Not impossible, perhaps, but unlikely. Tell me, how did you and your stepfather get along."

Michael gave him a long, level look. "Do I need a lawyer?"

"Not yet," the inspector said. "Let me explain a few things to you. First, there have been three prior complaints made against Janek Pryor by the parents of young girls. All three families had financial difficulties prior to these complaints, which curiously then vanished and all three complaints were dropped. You have two younger sisters." The inspector paused and raised an eyebrow. Michael shrugged again, at which the inspector gave a faint grin. "Lord Pryor is an influential man. His son's behavior has been a trial to him but the dead can no longer misbehave. Lord Pryor would not appreciate his son's memory being dragged through the mud. He would prefer that this incident be put behind us as soon as possible. So,"—the inspector's lips thinned and his eyes grew sharp—"I'm going to offer you a deal.

"The conscription lists have recently been posted. The Imperial navy is expanding. The marine corps is to be enlarged. There is trouble of some sort on the frontier." The inspector frowned. "There is always trouble of some sort on some frontier. For the current year, our world is obligated to provide over twenty thousand young men and women for the Imperial forces. The military needs men who are clever and willing to assume risk, who can evaluate a situation and take decisive action. Does that description fit you? I think it might."

The inspector raised an eyebrow and waited. Michael said nothing. The inspector shrugged. "You, young man, have recently undergone a burst of patriotic fervor. You are searching for direction, for a goal, and you have decided that the Empire's service will provide you with what you have been seeking. You are going to join the navy and your stepfather's unfortunate demise will be recorded as a sad, tragic accident. Do you understand?"

Michael cleared his throat. He looked around the room and slowly, a grin crept over his face. "*Ave, Imperator,*" he said. "I think the marines would suit me better."

The inspector examined Michael's face and gave an abrupt nod. "An excellent decision," he said.

Chapter 7

"Where are we going?" Curly asked.

That was a good question. Michael was still thinking about it. Despite his reservations regarding the 'mission' that Romulus had assigned him, he still considered himself, somewhere deep inside, a soldier. The Empire that he had served no longer existed but a new Empire had arisen to take its place. On some level, Michael felt that his obligation had long since been fulfilled. On the other hand, he needed something to do that he felt like doing.

One of the things he had purchased before leaving Baldur was an atlas of known space. The current Empire consisted of almost five hundred worlds, Reliance, the founding world being the richest and most populous. Most of the Imperial bureaucracy was situated on Reliance but the Emperor's palace had only recently been moved back to Earth, to a dusty, windswept island that used to be called 'Manhattan' and used to be, many thousands of years ago, the heart of the richest city on the planet. Now, Manhattan, like Earth, was largely abandoned, a polluted, radioactive wasteland.

The Prime Minister and Parliament had apparently decided to reclaim the ancient homeland of humanity and depositing the Emperor and his court on Mother Earth seemed a triumph of public relations. It also kept the Emperor and his meddlesome aides isolated, a useful situation from Parliament's point of view.

"First, we have to sell our cargo," Michael said.

Curly grunted. "Where?"

"Pick a world. Anyplace you've always wanted to go?"

"You serious?"

Michael shrugged. "It's a big universe. One world is as good as another." And of course, he didn't actually *need* to sell the cargo. The ship was largely self-sufficient and he had enough platinum, gold and jewels aboard to purchase whatever they wished for many years to come.

The Merchant's guild on Baldur had suggested three corporations that manufactured high end women's clothing and would be happy to purchase his spider silk. Michael had taken the credits and traded them for the fur of a giant, modified sable that was even softer than the spider silk and warm enough to protect against the coldest winter. In the end, there were enough synthetic substitutes available that the fur wasn't worth much more than he paid for it but it was a rare, specialty item and should at least make back the investment.

"I've always wanted to see Bali Hai," Rosanna said. Rosanna, like Curly, was large. She deftly slid an omelet from a frying pan onto a serving plate and split it into three parts, then set two plates in front of Curly and Michael. The omelet was cheesy and flecked with bacon, garlic and red pepper. Michael cut off a small portion and allowed his eyes to close in appreciation. Rosanna may or may not have been an artist, but an auto-chef, no matter how many recipes were programmed into it, did not have taste buds and could never adjust for the variation in individual spices and ingredients. Rosanna was a damn good cook. She was also good company. She was very pale, very blonde and very large—not fat, just large, with broad shoulders, ample hips and swelling breasts. She reminded Michael of a Valkyrie, beautiful, if your tastes ran to a woman who could crush you if she felt like it, but Curly obviously adored her. He constantly nuzzled her when he passed by, which seemed to provide Rosanna endless amusement.

"Not this trip," Michael said. "Let me amend what I just said; any world is not quite as good as another. If we want to sell the furs, we need a cold world. We can see Bali Hai some other time."

Rosanna took a bite out of her omelet and gave a minute shrug.

"How about Kodiak?" Curly said.

Michael sent a silent query to Romulus, who among his other attributes, functioned as the ship's primary brain. Romulus fed the requested information into Michael's interface and displayed it on the tiny grid implanted on his retina. Kodiak was a cold habitat with a permanent population adapted to the climate, a self-sustained artificial world, hollow and almost one hundred kilometers in diameter. It was a popular tourist destination, mostly for the skiing, which began high at the tops of enormous artificial mountains whose peaks hovered in the low gravity center of the habitat and ended kilometers down below.

"Fine with me," Michael said. "Romulus?"

Curly flicked his eyes to the side, where Romulus stood as usual near the table. The Second Empire had no robots as advanced as Romulus. Curly seemed to have trouble adjusting to its presence.

"As you have said, one destination is as good as another, so long as it is cold. I see nothing wrong with this plan."

"Great." Curly grinned, casting one last side-long glance at the robot. "How long will it take to get there."

"Four days," Michael said.

Four days later, they emerged from slipspace onto the edges of the Kodiak system and were immediately hailed. They responded and after a few minutes, were given instructions. Kodiak loomed in the blackness of space like a glowing jewel. The station was spherical, originally a large asteroid, it had been hollowed out and plated with a layer of steel and aluminum on the inner surface. From a distance, a row of ships could be seen attached to a series of docking bays around the station's upper pole. Their instruments recorded two hundred fifty-seven bays, more than half of which were occupied.

As instructed, the *London* drifted into their designated landing area, grapples were attached and a flexible loading bridge extruded from the station and attached to their airlock. "Ready?" Michael asked.

Curly nodded, wide eyed. Rosanna merely smiled, hefting a luggage pack over her shoulder.

They were met inside the terminal by a clearance team, who asked a few perfunctory questions, scanned them for weapons, which failed to detect the flexible plastic blade embedded in Michael's forearm and gave them directions to their reserved suites. They took an elevator that brought them down toward the asteroid's center and thirty minutes later exited through a large, domed building to what appeared to be bright sunlight amid a deep blue sky. In the distance, they could see buildings, forests, rivers, mountains curving up over their heads and vanishing into the distance. "Wow," Curly whispered.

So far, neither Curly nor Rosanna, despite her skills in the kitchen, had been called upon to do anything useful. Still, Michael had found that he liked having them around. Both of them seemed grateful to be off their home world. They cleaned up after themselves and didn't complain. They spent a lot of their time alone in the rooms that they shared. Michael tried not to think about what two such ungainly bodies might be doing in there, but the mating of grizzly bears came vaguely to mind. He winced at the thought and tried to banish the images. He just hoped that they didn't break the bed.

Michael had no experience at being a merchant captain but he had a lot of experience in training soldiers. So far as he was concerned, Curly and Rosanna were under his command and they might as well be trained. Neither had complained, not that it would have done them any good. So far, they had spent hours on weapons and hand to hand. Both of them seemed to have an aptitude. Both had solid muscle under their bulk and were much faster than their size would have indicated.

"Come along, children," Michael said. "This way." He had never been here, of course, but the construction of such habitats had remained basically similar for over five thousand years. This one looked much like all the others that he had seen, all those centuries ago. Lights set on tethers gave the illusion that a sun shone in the sky. Rotating panels allowed for alternating periods of day and night, which, for reasons set deep in humanity's DNA, seemed necessary to prevent clinical depression.

They boarded a tube train and ten minutes later, exited into a spacious square lined with shops and restaurants. Above their heads, a mountain covered with ski slopes rose into the distance. Curly and Rosanna both stared at it. "When do we get to do that?" Curly asked.

"As soon as you want. Let's check in, first."

Curly nodded. A ten minute walk brought them to their hotel, where Michael had reserved a small suite for himself and a larger one for his two charges, the cost of which would be docked from their pay. They registered at the desk, were given key fobs and a small booklet describing the main activities and attractions that Kodiak had to offer. "Enjoy yourselves," Michael told them. "If I don't see you, don't forget, we're leaving in five days."

Rosanna nodded. Curly seemed not to hear him, staring around the spacious lobby. Michael smiled and headed for the lift. He was looking forward to a little skiing, himself.

Chapter 8

Basic training was no tougher than young Michael Glover had expected, which was very tough indeed. Still, he never felt abused or even singled out. The instructors were fit, hard eyed men and a few women who treated them all dispassionately. The ones who tried but couldn't keep up, perhaps a quarter of the total, were kept back to try again. The few who didn't try were quickly cashiered.

Michael was good at it. He had always been quick and strong. His reflexes were excellent. He liked to fight, though he found that he liked to fight less when the fighting turned real.

"Parker, rodents incoming from your left side."

Parker grunted, a sound that could clearly be heard by the entire squad through their suit radios. They were standing against the wall of a shattered building in the middle of a downpour two hours after midnight. Ordinarily, their suits' night vision would have cut through the dark but the rain was cold and muffled infra-red. Michael sighed. He crouched as low as his armor would allow and ran a zig-zag pattern across the street. He didn't bother with the steel front door but punched out a window and dived in. The room was empty. Small favors, he thought. He ran into the corridor, up two flights of stairs, kicked in a flimsy wooden door and inched his way up to the window.

From here, he could see the Tar-Ilyan troops massed around the corner from his men. "Three, two, one," he whispered, and sent a rocket propelled grenade down onto the enemy heads. He followed up with a burst of machine gun fire. The rodents, a third of their number blown suddenly to bits, the rest blinded by the sudden flare of the grenade, the bullets and the resulting smoke, began to fire aimlessly and to no effect.

Michael's squad plowed into the center of the rodent troops. The rodents had guns but they didn't have armor and in less than a minute, they were all dead, their dismembered corpses littering the street.

"You all right, Parker?" Michael said.

Parker was their newest recruit, just out of training. He looked up at Michael standing in the window and waved. "Let's get going," Michael said. He jumped out the window and floated down to the street.

The Tar-Ilyans had been given a chance. They had been told exactly what would happen if they did not stop hijacking cargo from Empire ships but their government had concluded that the Empire was bluffing. The costs of the ultimatum that the Empire had delivered, the Tar-Ilyan authorities decided, was too great. They failed to consider that some things were worth more than mere money, like the principle, often stated and always meant, that you didn't fuck with the Empire or we would kill you.

At other times and in other places, the certain knowledge that this was the simple, certain truth had pre-empted many more wars than the Empire had ever had to fight. Revenge was sweet but fear was a truly priceless commodity.

The squad ran down the street, destroying buildings at random, stopping for a few seconds at scattered locations to set mines under the dirt, just to remind the rodents that death could come from all directions and at unpredictable times to those who pissed off the Empire.

Ten minutes later, they reached the pickup point and marched into the transport. The hatch closed and the shuttle drifted upward. An hour later, they were back on the ship, safe.

"Corporal Glover, reporting as ordered, sir."

Commander DeLany, the ship's CO, looked him up and down with what might have been approval. It was hard to tell. "Sit down, Corporal," he said.

Michael sat in the single chair across from the desk. "I've been reviewing your record," the CO said. "It's impressive."

"Thank you, sir." Michael pasted an attentive, neutral expression on his face but inwardly, he cringed. Coming to the attention of high command rarely augured well.

"Tell me, Corporal, what are your goals here?"

Well, Michael was uncertain where this conversation might be going but that one fairly begged to be kicked between the goalposts. "To serve the Empire, sir."

The CO allowed a small smile to creep across his face. "Yes, yes," he said. "We are all eager to serve the Empire. I meant in a more personal sense. What are you trying to accomplish?"

Aside from killing the enemy and trying to stay alive? "Accomplish, sir?"

The CO frowned. "What are you trying to accomplish for *yourself*, Corporal? I'm talking about your future. What sort of career were you thinking about when you joined the marines?"

Mostly, trying to avoid a murder charge. Probably smarter not to mention such minor details to the CO. "I wasn't thinking that far ahead, sir."

The CO gave him a doubtful look. "Well, think about it now. In every class of recruits, there are a few who stand out, who are clearly better at what we do than the rest. You would appear to be such an individual. Your squadron has confidence in you. Your Sergeants approve of you. We try to identify such men and women early. Those few are offered the opportunity for..."—the CO smiled. Something about that smile disturbed Michael—"special training."

Michael stared at the CO. "What would this special training consist of?"

The CO leaned forward. "Let me explain."

Chapter 9

Two days after arriving in Kodiak, Michael sat at a table in an outdoor café next to a ski lift, sipping a cup of hot chocolat flavored with some spice he didn't recognize. He had sold the furs that morning for a little more than he had paid, ate an early lunch and then hit the ski slopes. He skied for a little over two hours before taking a break. Now, he sat and watched, considering whether he might prefer to go back to the slopes or maybe jump into one of the resort's many heated pools, or maybe just head back to the room and take a little nap before dinner. Somehow, though, he had the feeling that none of these pleasant ideas were going to happen, not at the moment, at least, because something far more interesting seemed to be taking place.

Romulus' voice was soft through his interface. "The situation is as you thought," he said. "I have gained access to the station's secure datanet. The figures are quite clear."

Michael sipped his hot chocolat and added a little brandy to the cup. *Supposedly* secure datanet, he thought. The security in Kodiak was generally excellent. They were all tall, fit young men and women who knew how to mingle with the crowd. They were unobtrusive. On the rare occasion when a guest had too much to drink and grew obnoxious, the situation was handled with quiet efficiency. They were also robbing the place blind. Not all of them, maybe not even most but from what Michael was able to determine, all of the newest, the ones who had been hired in the past year, were part of it.

He had noticed a certain animosity between the guards, nothing too overt but unmistakable if you knew what to look for. The newer guards seemed too complacent, too smug. The veterans' eyes would narrow, their posture grow stiff when certain of their colleagues walked by.

Michael had been trained to notice things. He noticed this. It seemed…strange.

The station had hired a new Security Chief about two years ago, after the old one retired. Little by little, the new Chief had brought in his own people. Nothing unusual in that.

Michael knew that men who fought together, men whose profession it was to deal with sudden and dangerous situations, needed to depend on each other, to trust one another. These men didn't. That was unusual.

Not that it was any of his business. Michael smiled as he sipped his drink. What to do? That was the question. Such conspiracies tended to go high up in an organization, with multiple layers of cover-up and denial. Michael could give a friendly little warning to the habitat's COO. That might get him some thanks, even a small reward. It might also get him killed, depending on who else was in on it.

He opened a secure channel to Romulus and gave him his instructions, then leaned back in his seat. Definitely a nap, he decided. Depending on what exactly Romulus found, he might need the energy for what came after.

Chapter 10

Michael Glover's transformation took almost a year. They kept him asleep for most of it. Retroviral therapy introduced the genes for high density sarcomeres. He grew stronger. His reflexes, already excellent, were enhanced. A small server was implanted in his skull, attached to the optic and auditory centers of his brain. His vision was extended into the infra-red. His corneas were replaced with gell-like lenses, improving his vision down into the microscopic. Tiny radio receivers were implanted into the bone behind his ears as well as tiny bladders sensitive to minute vibration, giving him enhanced hearing and allowing him direct access to the planetary web. An enzyme was added to his pancreas so that he could chew and digest anything organic, including wood. The genes for antivenins were inserted into his liver, so that no poison could harm him, and alveoli were added to his lungs so that he needed hardly any oxygen to breathe.

"Nothing that your armor can't do just as well, of course, but armor is conspicuous. You can't wear armor in the middle of a crowd unless you want the crowd to know exactly what you are." Michael nodded. Four other men and one woman sat next to him, listening to the lecture. They all paid close attention. Their lives had changed and they needed to know this.

Omega Force, that was the name of the unit. They were a combination of commando, plainclothes military police and when necessary, spy.

"This is not a decision to take lightly," the CO had said to him. "You'll be given a week to decide. Think about it. If you agree, there is no turning back."

Let's see...a significant raise in pay. Officer rank, though nobody but the other members of Omega Force would know it. The ability, within reason and with some restrictions, to choose his own assignments.

The mortality rate in Omega Force bordered on forty percent. High, certainly, but not much different from that of the regular troops. They were soldiers. They served the Empire and if they served well and with distinction (they all served well and with distinction, while they lived) they would retire rich, and could go on to further lucrative careers in private security or even government service.

He thought about it but he didn't need to think for very long and after the week was up, he gave the CO his decision.

"Excellent," The CO said. He rubbed his hands together and he smiled. Michael still didn't like that smile but he put aside his misgivings, took up the pen and signed.

Chapter 11

Jonathan Taylor was the COO of Kodiak, recently appointed to the position. He had arrived well after the embezzlement began and therefore, in Michael's judgment, was not likely to be a part of it. His background was superb. He had graduated second in his class, just a whisper away from first, from the foremost business academy in the sector and then was hired as a junior executive by Resorts Interstellar, the corporation that owned Kodiak, as well as three other habitats. Jonathan Taylor was still young but not too young. He was seasoned, experienced and accomplished. He was also, to Michael's eye, exhausted, harried and at his wit's end.

"And you are?" he said.

"My name is Michael Glover."

Taylor frowned at him. "You're a security expert."

"That is correct."

"You told my secretary that you had some information for me." It was a statement, not a question. Michael inclined his head. "Alright," Taylor said. "I'm listening."

Michael handed him a small, shielded box with an attached monitor screen. "It would be unwise to connect this device to your systems. Keep it isolated. Press the green button," he said. "Watch."

Taylor raised his eyebrows, took the box and pressed the button. He stared silently as a series of documents and figures marched across the screen. His face turned slowly white. Finally, as the screen went blank, he sank back in his chair. "How did you get this?" he asked.

Michael shrugged. "Your systems are not as tight as you think they are."

Taylor shook his head and swallowed against a suddenly dry throat. He looked sick. "What do you want?"

"Me? Nothing. I'm just giving you a friendly warning."

"People are rarely so friendly without expecting something in return." Taylor grinned crookedly. "So, is your expertise limited to snooping?"

Michael cocked his head to the side and considered the other man. He had been expecting this question. "Do you mean, am I willing to help you solve this problem?"

Taylor steepled his fingers together under his chin. "I was sent here because Kodiak's profit margins have shrunk over the past few years. Frankly, the situation didn't make a lot of sense. The population of this sector is expanding. Business has been good. Nobody was expecting embezzlement, certainly not on quite this large a scale.

"I'm faced with a dilemma. You're a stranger. You've brought me information that could be incredibly valuable or could be completely false. I can't figure out what you would get out of making this all up, but offhand and at a minimum, making me look like a fool might be worth something to my rivals."

Michael shrugged. "None of this is my problem."

Taylor stared at his face. "No, it's not, unless I hire you to resolve it. Then it becomes your problem." He raised an eyebrow. "If I can trust you."

"Are you offering to hire me?"

Taylor chuckled. "Not yet. I have some people I need to talk to, first. Where can I reach you?"

Michael gave him his codes. "Don't wait too long," he said. "I was intending to leave here the day after tomorrow."

Taylor nodded. "I'll be in touch."

A knock on the door two hours later came as no surprise. The two large men and one large woman standing in the hallway were exactly what Michael had been expecting. "Mr. Glover?" one of them asked.

"Yes?"

"I'm Nathan Gerardi. I'm a lieutenant in the Kodiak Security Police. This is Jeffrey Leopold and Megan Gaynor. Mr. Taylor would appreciate your coming with us. There are some people he would like you to meet." They were wary but not particularly nervous. Their heartbeats were steady. They seemed to be exactly what they appeared. Michael had reviewed the files on all security personnel in Kodiak. These were veterans and all three had good records. Apparently, Taylor had decided that Michael could be trusted, or at the least, he was hedging his bets.

"Certainly," he said.

They turned down a hallway which led to a public square with a row of shops on one side and a restaurant on the other. They were halfway across the square when Leopold murmured, "Uh-oh." Five men were walking toward them down the center aisle. They wore the same security uniforms as Gerardi and his team. The man in the lead saw them. A wide smile crossed his face and he slowed. "What's this?" he asked.

"Seymour," Gerardi said. "This gentleman has a business proposition for the Director."

"Really," Seymour said.

Gerardi shrugged.

"What sort of business?"

"The lucrative kind," Michael said. "The company that I represent has established a series of alternative entertainment venues. Your habitat would be ideal for a franchise. The Director seemed interested in my preliminary proposal."

Seymour blinked at him.

Gerardi cleared his throat and frowned at his interface. "The Director's waiting," he said.

Seymour stared at Michael's face, then gave a minute shrug. He and his men walked on. Gerardi drew a deep breath.

"Trouble in paradise?" Michael asked.

"Seymour is one of the new guys. We don't always see eye to eye."

They resumed walking. Leopold turned to Michael. "What exactly is an 'alternative entertainment venue'?"

"Oh, you know: casinos, brothels, opium dens. Like that."

Megan Gaynor gave a barely audible snort.

"We already have a casino," Leopold said doubtfully. "I don't think the brothel idea is going to fly. It conflicts with the family friendly vacation theme. I think you can forget the opium den."

Obviously, Taylor had not told his team exactly what was going on. Just as well. Michael shrugged. "The Director seemed interested enough to agree to meet with me."

"It's not our business," Gerardi said. "We just do what we're told."

"I like your attitude," Michael said. "The world would be a better place if more people had it."

Megan Gaynor gave another snort. Michael smiled.

Chapter 12

"I can't afford an all-out war on this habitat," Taylor said.

Five people sat around the table: Michael, Taylor, Jonas Wells, a grizzled, middle aged appearing man in a Security Lieutenant's uniform, Leslie Sanders, a tall, blonde woman wearing an expensive looking business suit, who owned the largest private estate in the habitat and was a major shareholder in Resorts Interstellar, and Brady Lanier, who had been introduced as the Captain of an Empire corvette that had docked three days previous for shore leave. Lanier appeared to be about thirty years old, though the age at which a citizen of the Empire appeared was most often a matter of choice rather than biology. Sharp eyed and well built, Captain Lanier smiled readily, sat back in his seat and said very little.

All of them knew each other, even Lanier, whose ship had docked at Kodiak twice before in the prior three years. None of them knew Michael, which did not disturb him. It was nice to have your own ship and to be able to leave other peoples' trouble behind. This was Michael's problem only if he wanted it to be so. "Mr. Glover has done us all a favor but we have no reason to trust him," Wells said after Taylor's brief outline of the situation. He said it dispassionately, without anger or emotion. Leslie Sanders grimaced and looked down at the table. Lanier remained impassive.

Taylor frowned. "Do we have any secrets?" he said. "Kodiak is owned by a private corporation that pays its taxes and doesn't want any trouble. The fact that Mr. Glover has volunteered this information is reason enough to include him."

"How did you get it?" Wells said.

"My software is more advanced than yours. It wasn't hard."

"Your hardware is more advanced, as well," Lanier said. "I've never seen a ship like it."

Michael shrugged. "It's a big galaxy."

Lanier sat back, frowning.

"Let's go on," Taylor said. "It's my call."

Jonas Wells grimaced. Sanders nodded. Lanier sipped from the cup of coffee sitting in front of him on the table.

"So," Michael said, "You can't afford a war but I don't see how you're going to avoid one. Not if they choose to fight."

Taylor gave a frustrated sigh. "Yeah," he said. "I know." He pressed a button and a holograph lit up over the table. "Gregory Cabot, the current head of Kodiak security. According to the information provided by Mr. Glover,"—Taylor smiled wanly in Michael's direction—"all of the men and women hired by Gregory Cabot over the five years since his arrival are engaged in either embezzling funds or in intimidation of our other personnel, this number comprises fifty-seven of our one hundred and three person security force." A second figure appeared above the table, glowing in mid-air. "Harold Crane, our CFO. He assumed his position here one year before Cabot's arrival." A third figure appeared. "Leonard Rivas, Chief of IT. Apparently, all three of these individuals have been conspiring to skim approximately 0.23 percent from every transaction that takes place in this station."

Leslie Sanders frowned. "Who are these people? Are they doing this on their own or are they working for somebody else?"

Taylor sighed. "It gets worse," he said. He pressed another button. A figure of an elderly man with a sad face appeared. "Jordan Kent recently passed away. He was four hundred forty two years old." Taylor shrugged. "Natural causes, or so it was presumed. His last wife died over a century ago. He has no children or any other natural heirs. Somehow, his property has been transferred to a charitable trust. The trust, once you dig beneath the surface of multiple ownerships, appears to be administered by this man." A small man with sandy hair and a wide, satisfied smile, wearing a large gold ring and an expensive looking suit appeared in the air. "Paul Prescott Jones; he moved into the estate about six months ago. A very large transfer fee was paid to Rivas, Crane and Cabot." Kodiak, while constructed and managed by Resorts Interstellar, had sold off most of the habitat's real estate over the years to private individuals. The properties ranged from one bedroom vacation rentals to estates covering nearly a hundred hectares of land.

"Oh, crap," Leslie Sanders said.

"What is their end point" Lanier asked.

Taylor looked at Lanier and frowned. Michael nodded. It was the obvious question. "Robbing us blind, apparently," Leslie said.

"It may be more than that," Lanier said. "They've built up their forces to the point that an armed takeover of the habitat might be possible."

"That makes no sense," Taylor said. "Even if they could do it, the Empire would take it away from them." Resorts Interstellar was registered in Columbiana, a prosperous Earth like world that had been settled by the First Empire, came through the Interregnum with most of its infrastructure intact and had eagerly rejoined the nascent Second Empire.

Lanier shrugged. Lanier, Michael thought, perhaps knew more than he was saying.

"Will you help us?" Taylor asked Lanier.

Lanier leaned back in his chair, looking pensive. "I can observe. I can't take action unless Imperial interests are threatened. Usually, that means armed invasion by an outside force. Treason would also count, but so far, this looks like an internal criminal affair. I don't think so." He shook his head.

"Part of your mandate is to maintain order," Taylor said.

"True, but embezzlement and corruption do not necessarily threaten the public order. So far, this incursion, if you can call it that, has been entirely peaceful."

"How about you?" Taylor asked Michael.

Michael turned to Lanier. "How many are in your crew?"

"Fifty-three."

"More than enough to make a difference, if they were allowed to fight."

Lanier shrugged. "If they start shooting, my crew and I will respond appropriately. Otherwise, I have no desire to be cashiered."

Leslie Sanders looked first at Lanier, then at Michael, frowning. Jonas Wells shrugged.

"I'll do what I can," Michael said.

"And I'll extend the crews' leave for as long as I can," Lanier said. "Let's see how it plays out."

Chapter 13

Paul Prescott Jones had inherited a fortune from his father, who had inherited it in turn from his father, who, along with his brothers, had founded a successful shipping company. The latest Prescott Jones had done nothing to grow the company but had not been so stupid or so careless as to endanger his principal source of income. There were, after all, other members of the Prescott Jones dynasty. His uncle, Jonathan Prescott Jones was CEO of the corporation. Prescott Shipping had suffered its ups and downs over the years but had prospered under the current leadership for over a generation. That was more than good enough for Paul Prescott Jones. Let people run the business who knew what they were doing and liked doing it.

So far as Michael and Kodiak Security could determine, Paul Prescott Jones spent his time enjoying himself. There was nothing at all in his background to suggest a secret criminal career.

Neither Curly nor Rosanna looked like undercover agents, though Michael was entirely aware that undercover agents could look like anybody at all. "I don't know," Curly said. "It sounds dangerous."

Rosanna smiled. "I'll do it," she said. "No reason not to."

Curly grunted and shrugged.

Paul Prescott Jones' estate sat under a dome, which kept the ambient temperature nearly fifteen degrees Celsius above the Kodiak norm. He employed a weekly janitorial, landscaping and pool service.

"We could use our own people," Jonas Wells had said.

"True," Michael replied, "but for the moment, I would rather keep them out of it. We don't know how far your men have been penetrated, if at all."

Wells sniffed but didn't argue further.

Curly was good with machinery and he knew how to mow a lawn. Rosanna made a hefty but perfectly competent cleaning lady. "Don't take chances," Michael said. "Just do your jobs. The automatics will take care of the rest."

On a crisp, sunny afternoon, while Paul Prescott Jones was out skiing with his two children and his current mistress, Curly and Rosanna went in with the cleaning team. One or two of these gave them curious glances but there was a lot of turnover in their business and curiosity did not extend so far as suspicion. Curly mowed the lawn and trimmed the hedges. Rosanna fluffed up the pillows, made the beds and re-stocked the dispensers. As they worked, a series of almost microscopic recorders drifted off their clothes and lodged themselves into the corners of the house and yard. For two days, the recorders would transmit everything that they saw and heard. Then they would go dormant. They could be re-activated twice before their power was exhausted. If not re-activated within four weeks, they would degrade into tiny, formless blobs.

At the same time, so high above the dome that it could not be seen with the naked eye, a drone hovered, its cameras focused on the spacious estate of Paul Prescott Jones.

The same group sat around the table, with the addition of Jessica Izumi, Taylor's Administrative Assistant. "We don't need a warrant," Jonas Wells said. "Most people don't know it, but a habitat doesn't have laws. It has regulations. A habitat is neither a world nor a nation; legally, it's a ship. The laws of the planet of registration, in this case Columbiana, are supposed to apply, but like most planets, Columbiana doesn't want the headache of trying to administer far-flung motes of so-called civilization that are light-years away from its own territory. Basically, the COO acts just like the captain of a ship. He can declare anything legal or illegal that he wants, so long as the Corporation supports him."

It was different in the time of the Empire, Michael reflected. Imperial law had applied equally to every Imperial subject, wherever he happened to be; and every human being on every human settled world was a subject, along with every member of every allied race who had petitioned to join the Empire.

It made the job easier, however.

Paul Prescott Jones was as dirty as they came. No idea why. No idea how. God knows, he didn't need the money. Maybe he needed the thrill. He wasn't a stupid man, not exactly, but he wasn't making a lot of effort to keep his activities hidden. Probably, he had gotten away with it for so long, his position in society so privileged that the idea of being called to account was beyond his comprehension.

Or not. Maybe he was just stupid, or maybe he had stupidly listened to other people's assurances and assumed himself to be invulnerable.

Embezzlement, it turned out, was the least of it.

"Treason?" Michael asked.

Lanier puffed up his cheeks and gave a small shrug. "I think we can consider it armed invasion," he said.

It was more than just embezzlement, and it went beyond the borders of Kodiak. Piracy had been increasing in this sector. Ships had vanished, their crews and passengers abducted, killed or enslaved. Prescott Jones did not know the full extent of it. He was in charge of the operation on Kodiak and he sent a message now and then, pointing out ships that could easily be taken, but that was all.

Romulus whispered in his ear. "A text message has just been sent from Jessica Izumi to Gregory Cabot, Harold Crane, Leonard Rivas and Paul Prescott Jones. It reads, 'Code Red. Act Now.'"

"I have an idea," Michael said.

Wells and Lanier looked at him. Leslie Sanders raised an eyebrow. Michael rose to his feet. "Give me a minute. I'll be right back," he said. "Nature calls." He walked around the table and as he passed Jessica Izumi's desk, he grabbed her by the back of the neck, pulled her away from her keyboard and held her up by one hand. "What exactly is *Code Red*?" he said to her.

All of them were staring. Jessica Izumi's face was white. She compressed her lips in a thin line and shook her head.

"Romulus?" Michael said.

Romulus' voice issued from the overhead speaker. "The forces loyal to Gregory Cabot have left their barracks. They are preparing to attack the security agents still under the command of Lieutenant Wells."

"How much do they know?" Michael said to Jessica Izumi.

"You can kill me," she said. "I'll tell you nothing."

Michael sighed. "I'm afraid that you just got that all-out war you didn't want."

"Fuck," Taylor muttered, and reached for his phone.

Chapter 14

Michael dropped, rolled and fired off two quick laser bursts.

It was two hours later and fighting raged throughout the habitat. The good guys, warned by Romulus (though Romulus' robotic nature was, for the moment at least, being kept secret from Michael's erstwhile allies) and supported by Captain Lanier's forces, had responded more quickly than Gregory Cabot and his men had expected. Seventeen of Jonas Wells' officers had died in the initial attack. Romulus had taken command of the habitat's major functions, including the surveillance system. He had managed to lock twenty-two of Cabot's men in their barracks. Another fifteen had died in an attempt to take control of the port facilities when Romulus opened the airlocks to the vacuum of space.

He would have expected Cabot's men to give up once the writing on the wall became clear. They were mercenaries, after all. They were paid to fight but they weren't paid to die, not for nothing. That was usually the trouble with mercenaries; the mercenary code required a minimal level of commitment, but their hearts were never in it…except apparently not this time. These mercenaries seemed to have a different sort of code. They were fighting to their last breath.

The armor Wells had supplied him with was largely inert, nothing like the powered suits he had worn all those centuries ago, but it served its main purpose of protecting his arms, legs and torso from laser bursts and might even stop a bullet if the caliber wasn't too high.

"Incoming!" Leopold yelled.

A grenade floated toward him, seemingly in slow motion. He hit it with a laser burst, then ducked behind a pallet of crates as shrapnel sprayed out and around the cargo bay.

Jessica Izumi had presumably given the chief bad guys Michael's name. Any search through the web that they tried to conduct would tell them exactly nothing about who Michael was and where he came from, but that very lack of information would tell them more than he wanted them to know, as would the fact that he had docked in Kodiak with a private ship of unknown derivation and abilities.

If he was going to fight, it might as well be here, where he could prevent any attempts to hijack his ship. Lanier had refused to allow Michael to accompany the marines. Michael didn't blame him. They were professionals and Michael, so far as they knew, was an amateur. Wells had not been so picky. Wells had figured that they needed all the help they could get. If Michael got his head blown off, it was by his own choice, and he might at least serve to distract the enemy.

A rattle of bullets stitched a sudden line of holes in the crate above his head. Time to move. A small squadron of corporate troops flanked him on either side. He raised a hand, gave a signal and rolled left. The rest of the squad zig-zagged across the room, laying down a line of covering fire. The enemy crouched behind a series of metal shipping containers. They had no way to tell how strong Michael really was. He jumped, grabbed the top of the container, worked his way close to the opposite edge and threw down a series of crackers containing tranquilizing gas. He followed these with a smoke grenade. His augmented hearing could pick up at least two bodies slumping to the floor. Two others ran out from between the crates where Gerardi, Leopold and Megan Gaynor were waiting for them. They never had a chance. Neither tried to surrender. They made one last attempt to raise their rifles and died in a hail of gunfire.

The sudden silence was profound, almost eerie. Gerardi gave Michael a long, speculative look. Leopold shook his head. Megan Gaynor smiled, a slow, wide and smoldering smile, a smile that promised many things. He smiled back.

Chapter 15

"Orgies are a little tacky, don't you think?" Megan Gaynor stretched her arms over her head and grinned at him. "They do relieve the tension after a shootout, but I've come to prefer my sex one on one, or one on two at the most. I like to concentrate on what I'm doing."

They had concentrated pretty hard only a few minutes before, Michael thought, and truth be told, he was almost ready to start concentrating again. Lazily, he leaned over and kissed her on the lips, which she lazily returned, then he let his tongue trail down over her neck and nuzzled at her breast.

She gave him a sly smile. "The post-mission orgy is a tradition in some units. Nobody is forced to participate, at least officially, but if you don't, you might not be thought of as one of the guys. How did it work where you come from?"

And there it was: how did it work where you come from? And by the way, where do you come from? The implied but unspoken question. In Michael's time, sex between colleagues was frowned upon, as it tended to lead to a breakdown in discipline. It happened, but you better be discreet about it and never, ever let it interfere with the job. Megan Gaynor was looking at him, expecting an answer.

"I've never been to an orgy," he said.

"No?" She raised an eyebrow. "Not even one?"

"Not even one."

She shrugged. "They do broaden your horizons, though. Makes you a little more accepting of people who might not be just like you. For instance, I always thought a guy with a lot of hair on his chest was kind of gross until I found myself fucking one. Then it didn't seem to matter. Opens your mind." She stretched again. Megan Gaynor had a firm, tight body with a scattering of freckles and a couple of scars across her abdomen. She had proven to be good company, and not just in bed, though her talents in bed were truly exceptional. Probably that open mind.

"Fuck me again," she said.

"Yes, Ma'am." He smiled and did what he was told.

Two hours later, he met with Taylor, Wells, Lanier and Leslie Sanders. "We wanted to thank you," Taylor said. "You bailed us out of a very bad situation."

Michael was in a good mood. All's well that ends well, and all that. He was quite happy to accept the *de rigueur* thanks of the grateful populace and fly off into the sunset. Not that the operation was an unqualified success, but still…

Cabot, Crane and Rivas were gone. The airlocks had manual overrides, deliberately placed in case of a catastrophic system failure. The three, along with six other men, had donned pressure suits, opened an airlock and jetted across the habitat's surface to a midsize ship whose ownership could not now be determined. They had steered the ship out to the transfer point at the edges of the system, entered slipspace and vanished from the habitat's detectors. Romulus had been aware of this activity but there was nothing he could do to prevent it. By now, Cabot and his associates could be anywhere.

Four of Wells' men had been sent to arrest Paul Prescott Jones. He waited for them in his study and as they trooped into the spacious room, raised a cup of tea to his lips, smiled at them gently and took a sip. The tea proved to be laced with a quick acting nerve poison. He died with the same smile on his lips and never said a word.

The rest of Cabot's men, the ones who survived, knew nothing. They were exactly what they appeared to be: low level mercenaries.

"I've transferred a thousand credits to your account," Taylor said. "Consider it a reward. You've saved us a lot more than that."

More than he had expected, a lot more, actually. "Thank you," Michael said.

"Where are you going next?" Taylor asked.

Michael pondered the question. "I don't know," he finally said.

"Are you interested in a job?" Lanier asked.

"A job?" He frowned. "Probably not. What exactly are you proposing?"

Lanier looked at Taylor and the rest, then said, "I think we should discuss it in private."

Taylor frowned, thinking this over, then shrugged. Wells appeared relieved, though he tried not to show it. Wells had done an excellent job in a difficult situation and was probably hoping for a promotion. He didn't need any competition from some mysterious stranger.

Leslie Sanders was looking at him with a frown on her face. He wondered what she might be thinking but it didn't really matter. Tomorrow, he was out of here.

"So," Lanier said, "drink?" They were sitting in Lanier's stateroom aboard the *March One*, Lanier's corvette. It was a small ship and Lanier's office was cramped, without even the illusion of a window to brighten the view.

"Sure," Michael said. "Why not?"

Lanier poured a clear brown liquid into a glass, handed it to him and waited for him to take a sip. Brandy, and better than he had expected, not that he was a connoisseur. "Excellent," he said.

Lanier smiled. "I'll get right to it. You have a ship of unknown but obviously advanced capabilities, more advanced, frankly, than any ship that the Empire currently possesses. What else do you have?" He paused, waiting for Michael to speak.

Michael took another sip of the drink. Alcohol, various flavoring compounds, all natural, and nothing else. He wouldn't have been surprised at something a bit more psychoactive, something that might have released his inhibitions or even compelled him to answer the other man's questions. He would have smelled and tasted anything amiss, of course, but Lanier would not have known that. He might have suspected it, though. Michael shrugged and savored his drink.

Lanier grinned. "The Second Empire is determined not to repeat the mistakes of its predecessor. The First Empire lasted for four thousand years but in the end, it went down in flames. The Second Empire respects the rights of property, does not regard itself as the automatic and destined ruler of the galaxy and would prefer to expand through peaceful means rather than by conquest.

"My superiors will be very interested in my report of what happened here. They would obviously love to study your ship, to duplicate it if possible. They would like to know who you are and where you come from. Your world of origin and the technology that you possess could potentially offer a threat, or you could offer an opportunity." He paused again.

"Go on," Michael said.

"Some small segments of the First Empire still survive, or have managed to re-constitute themselves. The galaxy is wide and many alien races exist, some of which used to be human. Many beings have secrets that they would rather not reveal. So long as such beings do not represent an obvious threat, it is Empire policy to leave them alone. You are very far from the first such example that we have encountered.

"I am offering you a retainership. This is a routine arrangement and one that any Empire officer of sufficient rank is authorized to propose, a standard arrangement for newly discovered people and races. If you accept, you are required to do nothing except inform us of situations that might be threatening or otherwise require Empire attention and to send in periodic reports of your activities. You are required to be at least neutral in disputes regarding the Empire. You are not required to fight on our behalf. You are not required to surrender your ship or any of your possessions. You cannot be compelled to assist us in any way, though of course, such assistance would be greatly appreciated, depending upon the situation."

Really excellent brandy, Michael thought. He felt a nice mellow glow spread out, all the way to his fingertips. "What do I get out of it?"

"A series of contact codes which will allow you access to the commander of any Empire ship or base in any human occupied sector of the galaxy, and a small stipend." Lanier smiled. "Very small."

Not quite a spy, Michael thought. This didn't worry him. His experience in Omega Force had made him into an excellent spy. More like a paid informant, though he was not being asked to betray his family, friends, nation or world of origin. From the Empire's point of view, it was a cheap and easy way to gather information, costing very little.

"Sure," Michael said. "Why not?"

Chapter 16

Michael hated undercover work and avoided it as much as possible. For one thing, undercover work was boring. You went in, took some inconspicuous, low-level job as a cover and then sat there, doing your stupid, boring job, sometimes for months, occasionally for years, a secret asset that might never be used.

He was a pretty good assassin, though. The skills were actually similar but the time span was compressed, days or weeks instead of months. Get in, lie low for awhile, hit the target and then get out. It was an excellent job if you liked excitement and didn't mind killing people. Michael had scruples, though. He only killed the bad guys. His superiors knew this about him and didn't try to give him any assignments that he might find morally objectionable. They saved those for the psychopaths, of whom there were more than a few in Omega Force.

Dennis Reed, for instance, had been the governor of a moderate sized province on the very pleasant world of Tanis. He had been taking bribes from a slaver combine, delivering both the cargo manifest and passenger list of ships leaving the principal Tanis spaceport. Definitely a bad guy. Strangling him had been a real pleasure. There was something about the way the little fuck's eyes bulged out of his little red face that Michael found particularly appealing.

He had just finished his dinner in the mess hall on Cyrtis Base, Hyperion Command, and was sipping a cup of coffee when he saw her. She was tall and rangy, with curly black hair and deep blue eyes and she walked like she owned the place. Like him, she wore a one-piece uniform without insignia or rank. She saw him, grinned and walked over. "This seat taken?" she asked.

"No," Michael said. "Please sit."

She placed her tray on the table and sat down, then held out a hand for him to shake. "Marina Simmons," she said.

"Mike Glover."

She nodded and picked up her fork. She glanced up at him now and then while she ate but she said nothing until she had finished her meal. Michael understood. Sometimes, on a mission, you had to eat in a hurry, or eat things that you would otherwise find revolting. They had all learned to concentrate on their food. Michael had already emptied his plate but he felt no inclination to leave. He refilled his cup of really excellent coffee and nursed it while he waited for her to finish. After a few minutes, she patted her lips with a napkin, sat back and smiled. "How long have you been here?" she asked.

"Hyperion? A couple of months. I've been assigned to help train the next class. It's been a nice break. You?"

"They just woke me. I'm a sleeper."

He glanced at her in surprise. "I've never met a sleeper, not that I know of. I've always wondered why anyone would sign up for it."

She shrugged. "The Hirrill raided my home world. The city I grew up in was destroyed. I didn't have much to tie me down and I liked the idea of waking up into a better world."

"Has that ever happened?"

She grinned. "Not exactly."

"And so here you are."

Her smile grew wider. "Yeah."

"How long?"

"I've had four missions since I first went under. Altogether, about twenty-six years."

"Any surprises?"

She sat back, picked up her coffee. "Things haven't changed as much as I thought they would. The comp systems are smaller. The ships are a little faster. The base is different, of course, and the city. They're both bigger than they used to be."

"It sounds like you'll need somebody to show you around."

She grinned. "Are you volunteering?"

He liked her smile. He liked everything about her, actually, oval face, pert nose, sharp, amused eyes, long, rangy body, curling hair. "Yeah," he said.

"Okay," she said.

The Sleeper Corps was a division of Omega Force. The deal was that you could resign from Sleeper at any time, and sooner or later, most of them did, making friends, forming attachments, finding people and places that they preferred not to leave. Or sometimes, it was the opposite impulse that drove them to drop out, when they found themselves so far removed from the world that they knew, so far from everything known and familiar that they couldn't bear to continue.

They moved in together a week later. A week after that, Marina turned in her papers. She requested a training assignment, which was granted. They were happy but both of them knew that their situation was temporary. The Service had invested too much time, effort and money training them. They were both too valuable for permanent non-combat roles and the situation on the frontier was changing rapidly. The Hirrill were making more and more incursions into human controlled space. The war had been smoldering for decades, but was steadily growing in intensity. Everybody knew it, though nobody wanted to talk about it.

She took an assignment. It was either that or resign from Omega entirely and she wasn't ready to quit just yet. A month later, restless and irritable, he did the same. When he got back, she was waiting for him. He looked at her, lying in bed, wearing nothing but a grin and he drew a shaky breath. He felt a wide, dopy smile cross his face and realized right then that his life had changed, for the better he hoped.

Marina, thank God, felt the same way. They made plans to resign their commissions and retire to a world on the frontier but before they could do so, the Hirrill attacked. Most of Cyrtis base and the surrounding city was destroyed in the bombardment. He lay in the remains of their shattered apartment, covered by debris, with both legs broken, Marina's dead body clutched in his arms. He was near death from exposure and starvation when they finally dug him out and was in hospital for nearly two months, slowly recovering.

When he was finally discharged, he walked into headquarters and joined the Sleeper Corps.

Chapter 17

They had traveled far, straight out from the periphery of the Second Empire. It had been a whim, but Michael had no reason not to indulge his whims. Two thousand years ago, this sector of space had been peaceful and prosperous. Michael was curious to see what it had become.

Now, a city loomed beneath them, a series of ruins. Ancient buildings that used to scrape against the sky now slumped into merging piles of rubble. Trees, their roots digging into shattered concrete and steel, grew on top of the wreckage, interspersed with vines and thin, sickly shrubs. The broken city extended for kilometers on all sides.

A small village lay on the outskirts, a few hundred yards from where the rubble ended. A stone wall, perhaps three meters in height, surrounded the village, evidently constructed from chunks of fallen concrete.

The wall had not saved them. The village was a slaughterhouse. The bodies of men, women and children lay bloated and rotting in the sun.

"Recent," Michael said.

"The stage of decomposition indicates perhaps four days ago," Romulus said.

Curly's face was white. Rosanna's hands trembled as she stared at the screen.

"Notice anything strange, Curly?" Michael asked.

"Aside from dead people?" Curly shook his head.

"There are old men, old women and very young children. There are no young men or young women. What does that tell you?"

Rosanna got it first. "Slavers," she said.

"Yes," Michael said. "They took the ones who were valuable to them and killed the rest."

"Wasteful," Romulus said. "If they had left the survivors alive, the old would have raised the children and in a few more years, there would have been more young men and women for them to enslave. Why do this?"

"To terrorize the remaining population? To send a message? Because they enjoy it?" Michael shrugged.

"I'm picking up a few stray radio transmissions from the immediate vicinity," Romulus said. "Five hundred kilometers to the west, there are many more."

The world was listed on their charts as Janus 4-12: the twelfth moon of the fourth planet in the Janus system. Janus-4 was a gas giant rotating about its sun within the classic habitable zone. Its atmosphere was a mixture of poisonous gasses that contained mobile amoeboid blobs that were thought to be organic, though the First Empire had concluded that if the blobs possessed intelligence, it was a form incomprehensible to humanity. The twelfth moon, however, was only a little larger than Earth, with continents, oceans of mildly saline water and a nitrogen/oxygen atmosphere. It had been extensively terraformed and settled over five thousand years ago.

A contrail rose in the distance, a black metal speck on top of a bright orange flame with a thin, white tail that dissipated slowly in the atmosphere. They all silently watched the screen as it breached the atmosphere and vanished into space. "Primitive," Romulus remarked.

"So they have rockets," Michael said. "And they take slaves. What else do they do?"

"Let's find out," Curly said.

"Yes," Michael said. "I think that's a very good idea."

"What is this?" Rosanna asked.

They hovered over a large peninsula that jutted out into a tropical sea. The peninsula was covered by neatly laid out estates, each more than five hundred acres, with a large central house and multiple smaller buildings. One three story mansion, larger than all the rest, sat in the center of the peninsula. Next to this building was a stadium, covered by a sparkling retractable dome, large enough to hold perhaps five thousand people. An island off the peninsula's tip contained a spaceport, with ten small ships sitting on an open tarmac and a terminal building, seemingly empty at the moment, to the side of the field. A paved suspension bridge connected the peninsula to the island.

A ribbon of steel, rising over six meters in height and extending a little over two meters across, walled the peninsula off from the mainland. A tower with crenellated embankments and small windows rose every few hundred meters, spreading out on both sides of the wall. Kill zones, Michael thought, where attackers could be pinned between the towers. Armed soldiers, wearing military fatigues and carrying rifles, patrolled the wall.

It reminded him of something that he had read many hundreds of years ago. "*In Xanadu did Kublai Khan, a stately pleasure dome decree*," Michael said.

Curly looked at him. "Huh?"

"An old poem, once very famous, supposedly written during a drug induced hallucination." Michael sighed. "I may be wrong but offhand, I would say that this is an enclave for the wealthy elite. A pleasant, restful place where the Masters of the Universe can get away from the mundane cares of their overwhelming responsibility and relax in the company of their peers."

Curly frowned at the screen. "So now what?" he asked.

An excellent question. Michael was in possession of one of the most advanced ships ever built, a ship whose capabilities dwarfed those of what appeared to be a tin-pot interstellar Empire. Not that it was any of his business but he objected on general principles to people who casually slaughtered whole villages of helpless individuals and took the survivors as slaves. It annoyed him.

"Have you ever worn armor?" Michael asked.

"No," Curly said.

Rosanna had a determined look on her face. "There's always a first time," she said. "Just show us how."

"Romulus?"

The robot gave what appeared to be a tired, robotic sigh. "We serve the Empire, which means that we also serve the principles upon which the Empire was established. Such service is never ending."

Michael smiled. "Then let's get to it."

The ship's transformers could easily adjust stock composites to make armor of any size. An hour later, Curly and Rosanna shifted their feet uneasily in the airlock bay. Black scales covered their bodies, their heads concealed under dragon shaped black helmets, with red eyes and snarling mouths. Each of them carried a weapon that shot bursts of energy and looked like an enormous, black spear.

"Remember," Michael said. "The armor will augment every movement you make. I've set your strength settings to the lowest level but you can still break through stone walls or crush a man's ribcage with a punch. Best not to do so by accident."

They both nodded.

"Let's go then."

All three of them stepped off the deck, their AG kicking in. Romulus, who could directly interact with the ship's subsidiary brain, stayed behind in case they needed some sudden assistance. The three others floated toward the ground in triangle formation. Michael had Curly and Rosanna's controls slaved to his own and they landed behind a row of shrubs perhaps fifty meters from the house. The night was overcast but Janus covered three quarters of the sky and cast a dim silvery glow through the clouds.

The estate they had chosen fronted on the sea and was more isolated than most. Lights shone through the windows and music could be heard coming from an upstairs room. For a moment, they all stood still, listening, but the night was silent. Michael had thought it likely that the grounds would be patrolled but these people seemed to have no fear of invasion, evidently trusting to the wall across the peninsula and the soldiers that patrolled it.

They floated upward toward a second story balcony. Glass doors led into the house. The doors were locked. Michael gripped a handle and turned it. The lock snapped and the door eased open. They entered into a large room with high ceilings and a polished wooden floor. A small stage was set at one end of the room with a piano, chairs and music stands toward the back of the stage. The lights were off.

Michael walked across the room and into a wide hallway. At the end, light shone from underneath a wooden door. Michael walked up to the door, Curly and Rosanna silently following. The door was locked. Again, Michael grasped the knob, applied pressure and the lock gave with a small, audible snap. Curly and Rosanna flattened themselves against the walls on either side of the door. Michael opened it, ready to jump aside or dive to the floor but there was no need.

A man, thin, middle aged, naked and balding, lay back on a couch. What appeared to be an oxygen mask clung to his face, leading to a tank at the side of the couch. He was breathing in short, deep gasps. His eyes were glazed. A naked young woman knelt at his feet. She had tanned skin and long black hair. Her mouth was wrapped around the man's penis, one of his hands fisted in her hair as her head rose slowly up and down.

She saw them first. She gasped and raised her head, the thin man's penis flopping to the side. She rose to her feet and backed silently away, eyes wide. The man stared up at them blearily. "This isn't a good dream," he muttered. He inhaled quickly and a soft, unfocused smile crossed his face. His eyes fluttered.

"Can you understand us?" Michael said to the girl.

She nodded quickly. "Yes."

The First Empire had enforced the use of Basic, a derivation of ancient English. Most of the worlds the Second Empire had encountered still used it, but some had drifted away from the old tongue.

"What is this man's relationship to you?"

Her eyes flitted to the man on the couch and then back to Michael's face. "He is my owner."

Not surprising. "Who is he?"

She took in a short, quick breath. "Are you gods?" she asked. "The gods that my people have foretold will come down from the sky and free us?"

"No," Michael said. "No, we're not gods." As for freeing her people? Maybe. In the early days of the Empire, before their neighbors had learned to fear them, more than one alien race had taken human prisoners and turned them into slaves. Those alien races were now extinct.

Michael had always enjoyed freeing slaves.

The girl's shoulders slumped. A slow tear began to trickle down her face.

"Who is he?" Michael asked again.

The girl sniffed and wiped at her nose. When she spoke, her voice quavered. "He is Esau Kane, the Second Lord of the March."

The thin man still lay on his couch, the dreamy smile still fluttering over his lips. He laughed softly, reached over to the gas tank at the side of the couch and turned a knob.

"What is your name?" Michael said to the girl.

"We do not have names. My designation is F-17."

"Let me guess. Does that mean you are the seventeenth female slave in this household?"

"Of course. What else would it mean?"

Michael shook his head.

"So." The thin man grinned, his eyes suddenly sharp. He removed the mask from his face and placed it on top of the tank. He frowned at the girl. "Leave us," he said.

Rosanna shook her head and stepped in front of the door.

The man frowned. "I am not accustomed to being disobeyed."

Michael smiled. He reached out with his spear, touched the point to the man's chest and sent a crackling jolt of electricity through his body. It wasn't enough to harm him, just enough to focus his attention. He gasped.

"I think you misunderstand your position," Michael said.

They left an hour later, taking Esau Kane and F-17 with them. Rosanna carried the girl in her arms. Curly towed Esau Kane beneath him in a carry bag. The smaller man tried to struggle against his bonds. Curly ignored him. They rose, high above the peninsula, floated over the central mansion, more of a palace really, which they had been told belonged to Jaxon, the Twenty-Fourth Archon of the Diamond Empire, currently residing in the Imperial Palace in the Empire capital city of Malachite, on the world Tourmaline, in the Hermes star system, seven light years away.

Michael nodded at Curly, who seemed to hesitate for only a moment, then released the carry bag. Esau Kane struggled, his body contorting as he plunged through the air. A thin distant scream came to their ears as Esau Kane crashed onto the highest balcony of the Archon's mansion.

One down, Michael thought. A couple of billion to go.

Chapter 18

The Diamond Empire comprised eleven star systems, clustered within twenty light-years of the central star, Hermes. Their ships were primitive by the standards of the old Empire but had proven sufficient for the purpose of subduing their even more primitive neighbors.

The *London*, shielded from prying eyes, hovered in the atmosphere over the Archon's palace in the city of Malachite. The palace rose in tier after tier, spires and minarets and domes and flapping pennons, constructed of white and pink marble shining in the sun. It dwarfed the Imperial residence on Janus 4-12. A series of much smaller buildings, presumably government offices, surrounded the palace on both sides. A massive lawn stretched to a forest behind the palace, large enough to house herds of deer and wild boar. A huge wall surrounded the entire complex.

Malachite seemed a typical early industrial city. It had skyscrapers and residential neighborhoods and slums crawling with residents. Vehicles were forbidden in the central parts of the city. Palanquins carried by large, nearly naked men, presumably slaves, sedately traversed the streets. Men dressed in blue and gold robes walked along with nearly naked women at their sides. The women had collars around their necks and were held on golden leashes. Other women dressed in robes of silver and green similarly were escorted by large, muscular men, who also wore collars attached to leashes.

"Impressions?" Michael asked.

Curly grimaced. "They like to show off."

Esau Kane had been a vicious and confident man. He had five brothers and six sisters, seven of whom were older. He had demonstrated a talent for deception and sudden, unexpected violence and had mastered the art of poisonry at an early age. Three of his siblings still survived but Esau Kane, in the end, was named principal heir to his father's estate.

Esau Kane had told them everything he knew about the workings of the Diamond Empire before they killed him.

Their society was a meritocracy, in a way. The nobility fought and schemed and held the ultimate power beneath the will of the Archon but the Imperial bureaucracy, those who made the mundane, day to day decisions that actually ran the government, was chosen from the most competent and intelligent members of the commons. These were removed from their families before puberty, who were paid enormous sums for their purchase and were then gelded in the case of the males and sterilized if female, so that their ambitions would have no focus other than the well-being of the Empire. The bureaucrats lived in luxury but were kept close to the Archon in the Imperial Palace, and were always under guard.

The Archon ruled the commons with an iron fist but was circumspect with the nobility, all of whom kept private armies. On their own estates, the nobility ruled with an authority almost equal to that of the Archon.

A fun place, if your tastes ran to rape, brutality and casual sadism.

"What do you think?" Michael asked F-17.

When first brought onto the ship, F-17 had retreated into silence, confused by her new role, evidently unable to conceive of a life that did not constitute enforced service, sexual and otherwise. It took her a few days before she opened up and was willing to reveal her thoughts. Unfortunately, her thoughts tended toward the bloodthirsty, though considering the life she had lived, it was difficult to blame her.

She shrugged. "They have the power. They can do whatever they want."

"And when we free the slaves, what then?"

She frowned. "Then the slaves shall rule, and they shall grind their former masters under their heels. What else?"

What else, indeed? Michael sighed. "I was hoping for a bit more equitable a solution."

She gave him a scathing look. "You are foolish. Some rule. Some serve. This is the way of things."

Michael grimaced.

They say that a people gets the government it deserves. Michael had experienced many governments in his life, most of which the Empire had proceeded to conquer. Did those races deserve to be conquered? No, most people get the government that's imposed on them. Unfortunately, after a generation or two, most don't know the difference.

They say that a tiger released from captivity will pace back and forth to the extent of its cage. They say that freedom must be watered by the blood of patriots or it will inevitably vanish. They say that there is no tyranny so complete as a weak government. They say that power corrupts.

'*They*' say so many things, and so many of these wise sayings contradict each other.

Most revolutions fail to overthrow their governments. Most revolutions that do succeed in overthrowing their government fail to improve the life of their people, substituting one tyranny, often worse, for another.

It's hard to change and the hardest thing of all to change is a mind.

"We are going to make things better," Michael said. "Not worse."

F-17 gave him a cynical smile and shrugged. Curly and Rosanna looked at each other, then at Michael. "How?" Curly asked.

"I don't know yet," Michael replied. "But I will."

The Duchy of Norlin spread across the entire continent of Esterly, on the planet Regine-3, third world from the star Regine, the closest inhabited system to the capital, Hermes. Richard, the fifteenth Duke of Norlin had two sons. The oldest, also named Richard, was tall, strong, resolute and good with a sword. He was as strong as an ox and almost twice as smart. The youngest son, Roderick, was as tall as his brother, just as resolute and perhaps even better with a sword, also considerably smarter. Not that skill with a sword meant much in these days of interstellar ships, lasers and nuclear weapons, but sword fighting was a tradition, a part of their culture. A nobleman was supposed to know how to use a sword, and of course, the occasional challenge from a disgruntled fellow nobleman did require a response.

Of more interest to Michael was the way that Roderick Norlin treated his slaves. Oh, he used them, of course, as slaves were meant to be used. They picked up after him, cooked his food, groomed his horses and slipped his cock into whatever orifice he preferred at that particular moment, but he didn't starve them, mutilate them or even beat them (not without a very good reason, at least...), and he forbade his older brother and their mutual friends from beating them as well. For the Diamond Empire, this qualified as enlightened.

Their father also seemed to be a cut above the rest of the so-called nobility of the Diamond Empire.

"And you are?" The Duke of Norlin looked down at Michael from a large, carved and uncomfortable looking throne, his expression curious but not unfriendly. Michael and his retinue had arrived at the palace the evening before, claiming to be minor nobility from Valspar, the furthest world in the Empire, and produced papers confirming this claim. They had been shown to a suite of rooms and been told that the Duke would see them in the morning.

"Andrew Meyer, your Grace: fifth son of the Earl of Sandhurst."

Michael was the fourth person to be presented to the Duke, two of whom bore greetings from other nobility along with requests for temporary lodging on their journey to the capital. One brought samples of exotic gamebirds and spices from far off worlds and asked for a franchise to sell them in the Duchy, which was granted. The last was the son of an old friend of the Duke's, who would be fostered at Norlin for the season. The assembled court, perhaps forty men and women, along with their slaves, milled about the sides of the room. Most appeared to ignore these routine interactions.

"Sandhurst." The Duke frowned. "I regret to say that your father is unknown to me."

Michael shrugged. "My world is very far away."

"And what can we do for you?" the Duke asked.

"My father desires trade, my Lord. We are a cold world, very far from the center of civilization."

The Duke shrugged. "And what do you have to trade?"

Michael smiled. "That is yet to be established. We have furs and oils and hardwoods, all of which you may find to be of interest."

"Why have you come here? Why not the capital?"

"The capital is large and devoted to administration of the Empire. Imperial favor would certainly be useful but we are not likely to obtain it. The geldings collect taxes. They have no interest in trade. They have no need for trade." Michael smiled. "They have other ways to enrich themselves."

The Duke sat back on his throne and gave Michael a keen glance. "See my Chief Minister," he said. "He will help you."

Michael bowed. "Thank you, my lord."

Chapter 19

Roderick Norlin's body gleamed with sweat as he pounded on a crudely shaped piece of steel with a hammer. Among his other interests, Roderick Norlin was a smith. Among other trinkets, he made swords. As a member of the major nobility, it would have been beneath him to sell the wares that he made but as gifts, they were highly prized. Roderick Norlin made very good swords.

"So," Roderick Norlin said, "what have you discovered?"

Chief Minister Serlin was tall, thin, bald and stooped. He had graduated from the foremost University of the Diamond Empire with degrees in history and law, though he was aware from a very young age that in the Diamond Empire, 'law' was whatever the ranking nobility declared it to be.

Serlin was the fourth son of a cousin of a minor noble and though his family possessed little property and few retainers, his rank and family position had spared him from the usual castration and enforced Imperial Service. "Andrew Meyer is indeed the fifth son of the Earl of Sandhurst, a very cold and dreary place. However, according to my sources, Andrew Meyer is a very large, very shaggy young man who spends his days hunting and fornicating with his slaves. We have no pictures of the Earl of Sandhurst or his family. Could this young man be him?" Serlin shrugged. "He's the right size and if he's shaved his beard, maybe."

"Or maybe not," Roderick Norlin said.

"Or maybe not," Serlin agreed.

"What do you think of their proposal?"

"It makes sense. If it is legitimate, both of our people would be enriched by it."

"His retainers interest me. The two large ones stare as if they have never seen a court before, which I suppose is not surprising, considering where they come from." He smiled. "Or claim to come from. The other one, though, the beautiful young girl, did you notice her?"

"Of course I noticed her."

Roderick Norlin gave a thin smile. "She is a retainer, not a slave, and yet she never travels further from his side than the length of a leash."

Serlin frowned. "I didn't notice that," he said reluctantly.

Roderick Norlin grunted and the metal beneath his hammer glowed as sparks showered down from the anvil.

Before they first entered the Duchy of Norlin, their microscopic bugs had drifted over and down onto the palace and most of the nearby city. "Roderick Norlin is no dummy," Michael said.

"No," Romulus said.

"Do you think he's our man?"

Romulus stared at the screen and considered the question. "Considering the nature of this third rate little Empire, I don't think we'll find a better."

"No time like the present," Michael said.

Roderick Norlin opened the door to his suite and turned the light on. He stopped and a quick grin crossed his face. "How did you get in here?" he asked.

Michael Glover sat in Roderick Norlin's favorite chair, sipping a glass of his favorite whiskey. The window behind him was ajar, letting in the breeze. "Let's talk," Michael said.

"Yes," Roderick Norlin said. "I think we should." He poured himself a glass of whiskey from the sideboard next to the fireplace and sat down opposite Michael.

A nice room, Michael thought, barbaric in its way, the walls hung with ancient tapestries and an assortment of swords and knives. The floor was polished stone, clean, neat, immaculate. The high posted bed was covered by a silk duvet. Nothing in these rooms was out of place. Roderick Norlin was a man who liked things to be just so. Michael approved of that.

"You don't mistreat your slaves," Michael said. He said it with a grain of salt, as by any civilized definition, having slaves at all was mistreating them, without even considering all the other cruelties that the institution of slavery involved. The Diamond Empire, however, was not exactly civilized. *We have to make do*, Michael thought.

Roderick Norlin shrugged. "I'm not a sadist."

"No. That makes you unusual among the so-called nobility."

Roderick Norlin cocked his head to the side, raised one brow and sipped his whiskey. His eyes never left Michael's face.

Bull by the horns, Michael thought. He smiled and leaned forward and carefully placed his glass on the low table in front of him. "How would you like to be the Archon?" Michael said.

Richard Norlin the Younger, future Duke of Norlin, was the despair of his father, never more so than now. "You're drunk," the Duke said.

"I have reason to be," the younger Norlin slurred, and stared owlishly at his father. His brother Roderick kept his face carefully blank and said nothing. Michael, sitting next to Roderick at dinner, just below the Duke's high seat, kept a smile on his face and stolidly chewed his food.

So far as Michael was concerned, their business in the Diamond Empire was nearly done. After his initial meeting with Roderick, he had met privately with the Duke. Serlin had been called in to give assistance and advice, then Roderick had been invited to participate. Nobody had considered asking Richard. Richard, dimly aware that something was going on that did not involve him, resented this situation.

"You're asking us to change our entire culture," the Duke had said.

"That is correct," Michael replied.

"Why should we do that?"

"From the point of view of the Empire, the Second Interstellar Empire, which comprises over five hundred star systems and is far more technologically advanced than your own little Empire, your culture is an abomination."

The Duke grinned wryly. "Men of good will may have honest disagreements about such things."

"Don't expect much good will when the Empire discovers you. The Empire does not tolerate slavery. There will be no compromise or even discussion on this point, not at all."

"Hmm…" the Duke said.

"The Second Empire is less than fifty light-years away. It is slowly expanding in this direction. In the normal course of things, it will reach you in less than a century."

For the first time, the Duke frowned. "Normal?"

"I intend to tell them all about you. That may accelerate the process."

"Ah," the Duke said. He fingered his sword. "Not if we kill you."

"You are welcome to try," Michael said. "You might possibly succeed but if you do, then you, your sons and your retainers will very shortly cease to exist."

The Duke puffed up his cheeks in thought. "Can you prove this statement?"

"Go to the balcony. Look up."

Wordlessly, the Duke, Serlin and Roderick all rose to their feet, walked out of the conference room through the glass doors, trooped across the tile covered floor of the balcony and up to the rail. At first, they were greeted only by the sight of a sunny, cloudless sky. Then the air seemed to shimmer and slowly, the *London* appeared, over one hundred meters long, hovering over the castle. After ten seconds, the ship winked out.

"I see," the Duke said. "What keeps it from falling?"

"Anti-gravity."

"That would be useful," the Duke said.

"We think so."

"So," the Duke said with a wide smile. "Let us discuss your proposal."

Michael, or Romulus rather, would give the Duke of Norlin the secret of anti-gravity, of fusion generators, stasis shields and miniaturized lasers. As an added bonus, he threw in a supply of anti-agathics, enough to last the Duke, his most trusted advisors and his immediate family for twenty years. The average citizen of the Diamond Empire lived fewer than eighty years. The citizens of the Second Interstellar Empire lived closer to four hundred. "If you carry out your end of the bargain, we will supply you with the knowledge to make your own. Let this serve as an additional incentive. You will immediately declare it the law that slaves in your territories are to be treated humanely, and they will be paid a reasonable compensation for their work. Within five years, you will

71

institute systems whereby slaves can purchase their freedom. Within twenty years, you will outlaw the institution of slavery completely. You will form a parliament and give the common people enough representation in the political process that they will have no incentive to revolt."

"They may revolt, anyway. People sometimes do."

Michael shrugged. "Govern wisely. They will be less likely to succeed."

"These are ambitious plans. The Archon and the rest of the nobility will object," the Duke said with a smile.

Michael smiled back. "I don't think that I need to instruct you in how to play this game. You will have a lot of carrots and a lot of sticks. I am certain that you know how to forge the appropriate alliances and in less than twenty years the technological advances that we're giving you should enable you to take over the political system of this pitiful Empire. You personally will be registered with the Second Interstellar Empire as an asset. If they reach here before the transformation that we have discussed is complete, they will refrain from destroying you so long as you are moving things in the right direction."

"Twenty years," the Duke said.

"Twenty years should be sufficient."

Serlin, who had been listening without saying a word, puffed up his cheeks and nodded. Roderick nodded as well. "Yes," the Duke said. "I agree."

"You can be the Archon and Roderick will succeed you, or you may prefer to return to Regine and enjoy your well-earned retirement. That is up to you. The anti-agathics slow the aging process by approximately eighty percent. You are no longer a young man. In the normal course of things, you might live for another twenty years. With the knowledge and technology that we will give you, you should have another hundred, perhaps more. Use them wisely."

And so here they were, in the midst of a celebratory feast, though none of the assembled court knew exactly what it was that they were celebrating, and Richard Norlin was drunk, also surly. Richard resented being frozen out of his father's plans. Richard resented his younger brother, who seemed, as he almost always did, to be part of the circles of government that he, Richard, the rightful heir, somehow could never seem to reach (not, if he were being honest with himself, that he really wanted to), and most of all, he resented this effete, smiling stranger who came out of nowhere and seemed to have more favor with his father than he ever could.

Richard Norlin fingered his sword and he brooded, and finally, drunk, he rose to his feet. "You are a pretty thing, aren't you?" he said to F-17, who sat with Curly and Rosanna two rows down from the high table. "How would you like to suck my cock?"

The behavior of the nobility in the Diamond Empire did tend toward the crude, Michael thought. Unlimited power and all that, though Richard Norlin was perhaps a bit more crude than most.

F-17 cast a worried glance at Michael, who smiled at her and gave a tiny nod of his head. She gave an uncertain smile back and turned to Richard. "I am not pretty," she said. "I am beautiful, and I am much too good for the likes of you. I do not suck tiny noble cocks. I prefer a challenge."

Richard peered at her. His nostrils flared. He took a step forward. Rosanna rose to her feet, clutching a chicken leg with her left hand, and punched Richard Norlin in the head. He fell backward and slumped to the floor, unconscious. Rosanna sat down, took a bite out of her chicken leg, opened and closed her right fist several times, then picked up a glass of red wine and drained it. Curly gave her an awed, worshipful smile.

Silence reigned in the hall. The Duke sighed. "That idiot," he was heard to mutter. Roderick Norlin shrugged and picked up a chicken leg of his own.

Richard Norlin's chest rose and fell. He gave a huge, drunken snore. The Duke's eyes flicked to the side. Four retainers in the Norlin red and black livery stepped forward, lifted Richard Norlin's sleeping body and carried him from the room.

"Forgive my son," the Duke said. "He is impetuous."

"He is young," Michael said. "The young often are." This was polite, even diplomatic, since Richard Norlin, at nearly thirty years of age, was no longer young.

"Well," the Duke said. "Be grateful that he is not your problem."

"Thank you, your Grace," Michael said, and drained his glass of wine.

Chapter 20

F-17 had chosen a name for herself. From now on, she announced, she was to be known as 'Gloriosa.' Michael stared at her for a moment, cleared his throat and said, "Very well."

Curly and Rosanna glanced at each other. "Are you sure about that?" Rosanna asked.

The newly named Gloriosa gave a radiant smile. "I am certain. The name suits me."

They were sitting in the London's spacious galley, having just finished dinner. "I guess it's better than F-17," Michael said.

Gloriosa threw her arms out to the sides and exclaimed. "It is glorious! Like me!"

Richard Norlin, seated a little apart from the others and having said not a word throughout dinner, rose to his feet and left the room, his shoulders hunched. Michael frowned at his retreating back. So much for Richard Norlin not being his problem.

"He'll get over it," Rosanna said. "Leave him alone."

What a bunch of misfits, Michael thought.

The evening before they left Norlin, the Duke had asked to speak privately with Michael. He had been expecting a strategy session, perhaps an offer of formal alliance with the Second Empire, perhaps a request for further assistance somewhere down the road, something important at any rate. He was wrong.

"I would like you to take my son with you," the Duke said.

Michael stared at him. The Duke gave a tired grin. "Richard is heir to the Duchy but he no longer fits in here, not now, not under the current circumstances. And he knows it. This project that we are setting out on, it requires a cool head and good judgment, and it will go on for many years. Richard has never demonstrated either of those qualities." The Duke shook his head, rubbed his eyes and winced. "Richard's proclivities..." The Duke looked pained, almost embarrassed. "Well, we won't speak of them."

God help me, Michael thought. He wondered just what the nobility of this benighted little Empire could possibly consider perverse. He had an uncomfortable feeling that he was going to find out.

"Richard has grievances," the Duke said. "To some extent, those grievances are justified. I favor his brother because his brother can be counted upon but all Richard sees is that I favor his brother. I'm afraid of what Richard might do."

"So you feel that he'll get into less trouble as part of my crew? That's a very dubious assumption."

"I hope he might find a place that suits him, out among the stars."

"Wherever he goes, he will still be your heir. I don't think he's going to forget that."

The Duke shrugged. "If this venture succeeds, Roderick will be Archon and Norlin will be the least of his concerns. Richard can return. When I am gone, let him be the Duke of Norlin. If he makes mistakes, the Archon will be in a position to correct them.

"And of course, if this venture does not succeed, we will all be dead and Richard will be alive. Perhaps, if such is our future, he will be able to glean some satisfaction from that."

Michael winced. "On your head be it," he said.

"Thank you," the Duke said. "I am grateful."

Michael cracked a reluctant grin. "You should be."

They were three days out, heading toward the Pleiades, the closest star cluster to old Earth, which once upon a time had been a major center of art, commerce and invention, one of the richest sectors in the Imperial sway. Now? It lay more than seventy light-years beyond the borders of the current, Second Empire. What was out there? Michael was curious. They had nothing more important to do. Why not find out?

The fact that one of the brightest stars in the Pleides was Electra, Michael's home star system, did weigh at least a little bit upon the decision.

Just in case, they had picked up a cargo of perfumes, iridescent cloth that was similar to spider silk, spun by giant, mutated moths, and Norlin variants of cinnamon, saffron and black pepper. There might be something to trade for in the Pleiades and if not, they could always sell their cargo later. The Duke of Norlin had been happy to give it to them, in partial payment for the advanced technology that would (he hoped) allow him to conquer his own little portion of the galaxy.

They spent much of their time training. Curly and Rosanna were willing, even eager participants. Their size and strength gave them natural advantages but they both seemed to realize that skill and technique were even more important. They worked hard. Gloriosa had resisted at first, pouting and declaring herself an object of love and desire, with no wish to possibly mar the smooth perfection of her skin with bruises or even worse, scars. Michael had insisted, and the young girl proved to be surprisingly adept. She was agile and strong for her size, with quick reflexes, and when provoked, she possessed a killer instinct.

Richard Norlin also resisted, at first. He stayed in his room, feeling sorry for himself but within a few days, boredom drove him out. His face was haggard, his expression grim. He worried Michael. He participated fitfully, rarely smiling and went through the drills that Michael and Romulus assigned him but seemed to be holding back. The first time, he returned to his room as soon as the session ended.

Gloriosa watched him go, frowning. "Why did you bring him?" she asked.

"His father asked me to. It seemed like the best solution."

"For them, perhaps. For us?" She shrugged.

Since Michael had in the beginning almost as many reservations about including Gloriosa in his motley band, he found the word 'us' to be a bit presumptuous. He had to admit, however, that despite his initial doubts the former F-17 did fit in with the rest. Her rather rigid view of human nature could be off-putting but she was tough, didn't ask any favors and had a refreshing enthusiasm for life and new experiences.

"He feels lost," Rosanna said. "He's like a fish out of water. He has no place here and he knows it."

Gloriosa sniffed.

"Hopefully," Michael said, "he'll come around." He frowned. "And he has as much of a place here as any of you, if he wants it."

Rosanna had the grace to blush and nothing more was said on the subject.

Slowly, fitfully, Richard seemed to. He spent more time in the gym, lifting weights and running through the drills that he was assigned. The skills necessary to master a sword were similar to those required for hand-to-hand. Richard caught on quickly and even seemed to enjoy the exercise. He came to dinner with the rest of them and though he rarely spoke, he at least paid attention to the conversation. Occasionally, he even smiled.

"Where is Richard?" Michael asked.

Curly, Rosanna and Gloriosa were playing a game with colored ivory tiles. Gloriosa appeared to be winning. She shrugged.

"Haven't seen him," Curly said. Rosanna shook her head.

Romulus' voice issued from a speaker. "Richard Norlin is in the forward cargo hold."

The forward cargo hold contained a large assortment of miscellaneous goods, gathered from nearly a dozen worlds. Michael frowned. "What's he doing there?"

A holograph appeared near the ceiling. It showed Richard Norlin sitting on a bench in front of an electronic keyboard, his hands flying up and down the keys, head bobbing, shoulders hunched, his feet tapping with manic ferocity. All of them stared at the image. "Well, that's a surprise." Michael said.

Romulus didn't answer.

"Give us the sound," Michael said.

The sound crashed through the room: fast, precise, a perfect waterfall of notes.

They all listened for a long moment before Michael asked, "What is that?"

"*Piano Concerto Number 2*, by Franz Liszt," Romulus said. "A very old, very difficult piece."

Richard Norlin knew his way around a keyboard, that was for sure. Michael could barely believe it.

As the last slow note drifted off into space. Richard waited for a long moment, took a deep breath, nodded his head, once, twice, three times and then his fingers smashed into the keys. The sudden beat was loud, driving, rhythmic, and he sang while he played in a deep, bass voice, resonant and rumbling. The song was in ancient English, and barely decipherable, but the music spoke loud and clear, nonetheless.

All of them listened, amazed. Curly bobbed his head in time to the beat. Gloriosa's eyes grew wide. They listened without speaking until the piano tinkled to a final note, then Michael said to Romulus, "So what exactly are *blue suede shoes*?"

"Dancing apparel," the robot said, "worn on the feet. The song was an early classic of rock and roll, meant to convey the unfettered spirit of exuberant youth."

"He's good," Michael said. "He's very good."

In the holograph, Richard smiled fiercely, then his fingers once again moved deftly across the keyboard.

"*Whole Lotta Shakin*," Romulus said, "by Jerry Lee Lewis, considered by many scholars to be the most definitive and perfect example of the genre."

Rosanna's foot quietly tapped along with the beat. Gloriosa stared at the holograph with fixed intensity, her lips parted. At one point, she quietly moaned.

Who knew? Michael thought. Maybe he's not an idiot, after all.

Chapter 21

Electra-3 was barren, nearly dead. Where hardwood forests of oak and maple once rose, now only rotting stumps pushed their way out of radioactive sand. Ocean waves rolled over the crater where once stood the great city that Michael had called home. There was still life, though. Deep in the sea, fish still swam and on the land, mutated insects and giant rats fought for dominance. The birds were gone.

Michael sighed. He felt numb. His sisters had married and had children and then grandchildren. He had visited them, when he was able. They had been happy. He hoped that their descendants managed to escape whatever apocalypse had happened here. He shook his head.

Michael had deliberately kept his background and his origins a secret, even from what he was slowly beginning to think of as his crew. It wasn't that he didn't trust them, though he did not, in fact, entirely trust them. It just seemed wiser. Still, the others could see that he was profoundly affected by the images on the screen. They cast worried, sidelong glances in his direction and gave him space. And what, after all, was there to say? The devastation of Electra-3 had taken place well over a thousand years ago. Nothing remained but ruins and dust.

"There is an energy signature coming from the far side of the smaller moon, Chronos," Romulus said.

"Is there?" Michael raised his head. "Organic?"

"No."

Michael shrugged. "Take us there."

An hour later, they hovered over a metallic installation. It sat on a flat, airless plain and rose for almost a kilometer in a roughly pyramidal shape. Sunlight shimmered across its surface, seeming to change color in random patterns.

"What is it?" Curly said, awed.

"No idea," Michael replied.

The *London* suddenly shuddered. Romulus cocked his head to the side in apparent contemplation. "This might have been a mistake."

The patterns sweeping across the pyramid had gone still. Near the apex, a round hole dilated open in the pyramid's side and slowly expanded to over a hundred meters. The *London* drifted toward it. "What exactly is going on?" Michael asked.

"We appear to be caught in some sort of tractor beam," Romulus said. "It's drawing us inside."

"Fuck that. Nuke the place," Michael said.

Romulus said nothing for a moment. "I cannot. A force field is covering the outside of our ship, in conjunction with our own shields. At the moment, nothing can either enter or exit."

"Try the lasers."

A beam of green light shot out from the *London*'s prow and splattered against the pyramid in a shower of green sparks. "We cannot penetrate their shielding," Romulus said. "Not surprising. Their technology appears quite advanced."

Michael sighed. Curly and Rosanna exchanged worried looks. Gloriosa glared at the screen.

"Well," Michael finally said, "they haven't destroyed us out of hand, which means that they want something. Hopefully, we'll be able to negotiate."

"Probably they want to torture us to death slowly," Richard said. "That would be a lot more fun than simply blowing up the ship."

Michael gave him a disapproving look. "Let's hope not."

A few minutes later, the *London* settled to the floor of a gigantic chamber. Three other ships, all smaller than their own, one spherical and apparently of alien construction stood near them. Behind and above the *London*, the opening in the pyramid's wall contracted, then closed.

A soft, pearly light filled the chamber. Romulus, monitoring the ship's sensors, said, "The room is filling with a mixture of gasses, primarily nitrogen and oxygen."

"Any signs of life?"

"Nothing organic. However, numerous monitoring instruments are trained on our hull. Something is aware of our presence."

A few moments later, Romulus said, "The inflow of gasses has ceased. The atmospheric pressure is approximately Earth normal."

"That sounds like an invitation," Curly said.

Rosanna frowned. Gloriosa gave a wide, relieved smile and bounced a little on her feet. Richard Norlin looked grim, but then he usually did.

"Or a command," Michael said.

"The tractor beams are still fastened to the *London*'s hull," Romulus said. "We are unable to move from our current berth."

Michael shook his head. "They're not giving us a lot of choice."

"This installation obviously possesses tremendous power," Richard said. "They could have killed us at any time." They all stared at him. It was not like Richard to look on the bright side, and Richard's hopeful contention was an unproven supposition. The *London*'s screens had not been breached. Maybe they couldn't be.

Finally, Michael sighed. "They haven't tried to kill us and they've provided an atmosphere that we can breathe. It does appear that our presence has been requested, or at least will not be resented. We might as well see what they want."

Ten minutes later, they stood in the landing bay, covered in armor, all of them clutching black staffs. The airlock cracked open, the ramp extruded and they marched down to the floor of the chamber, which appeared to be some rigid, black composite. "Where to?" Curly asked.

A small, round, yellow light came on at their feet. They stared at it. The light began to move across the floor. They continued to stare at it. The light stopped. Michael took a step toward the light. It moved one step further away, then stopped again. "I guess we're going that way," he said.

They walked in single file, Michael first, with Romulus covering the rear. They followed the light, which moved at the pace of a moderate walk. Within two minutes, they came to the wall, made of the same dark composite, looming high above them. It dilated open, revealing another room, this one exactly twelve meters by twelve meters. "I suppose we could go back to the ship," Michael said, "but then what?"

"I see no real choice," Richard said. "At best, we are prisoners. It might as well be here as there."

"Anyone else?" Michael said. Curly and Rosanna looked at each other. Rosanna shrugged. Gloriosa shook her head. "Alright, then." He stepped into the room. The others followed and the wall closed behind them. Michael winced. "I was afraid of that."

Ahead of them, three openings appeared in the wall, swiftly expanding to over two meters in height by three meters in width. In the center of each opening was a rotating, blue circle of light. "Now what?" Curly said.

"I guess we're supposed to choose one," Michael said.

Romulus moved toward the circle on the left. He extended one arm and pushed it through the circle. He extended his other arm toward them and a hologram appeared in the air: a pleasant blue sky with a few high, fluffy clouds, a line of trees and a glint of water shining in the distance. As they watched, a flock of birds flew past. "This is what lies beyond the circle," Romulus said.

"I don't understand," Rosanna said.

"Shortly before the fall, the Empire had begun working on the construction of pocket universes. It would have been logical to place them here, on an isolated moon, out of harm's way, where they could be controlled."

"How big would they be?" Richard asked.

"If the theories regarding the Big Bang and inflation of our own universe are correct, such a universe could be as large as our own, or larger. This is only an entrance, it is not the universe, itself."

"There are two other circles," Michael said. "Where do they lead?"

Romulus appeared to shrug. Without a word, he walked over to the second doorway and extended one arm. A hologram appeared, a distant vision of stars shining in an infinite background. "Vacuum," he announced. "Empty space."

He withdrew his arm and went to the third circle. This time, a vision of a huge, gas giant planet appeared, pink and purple clouds roiling its surface. "The entry point is again in vacuum," he said, "in orbit around the planet."

"Well," Michael said, "I guess it's door number one."

"Do you think that these are three different entry points into the same universe, or three different universes?" Richard asked.

An intelligent question, Michael thought. No, Richard Norlin was not a dummy, not once his interest was engaged.

"Impossible to say," Romulus said. "I don't have enough data."

"Not that it matters," Curly said.

Richard shrugged and stepped through the first circle. The rest of them looked at each other, then Curly stepped through as well, Rosanna following, and then the rest. Michael found himself standing on a grassy meadow at the edge of a forest. Behind them, the blue circle glowed in mid-air, then winked out. Gloriosa sighed.

"There is organic life," Romulus said. He pointed toward the trees. "That way."

There were also radio waves and a high-frequency wifi network that seemed to blanket the entire vicinity with an even, sub-audible hum. Romulus, Michael knew, would have detected it as easily as himself.

A black bull, ten feet high at the shoulders, with curved ivory horns and a ring through its nose, emerged from the forest. It saw them, stopped, pawed once at the ground with a front hoof and charged. They scattered. The bull turned, raised its head to the sky, bellowed and then charged again. Michael raised his staff. A burst of red energy erupted from its tip. The bull's head fell from its body, a surprised look on its face. The body stopped, stumbled forward and fell to the ground.

They looked at each other.

"Not the most auspicious beginning," Michael said. "Let's go on." He pointed to a small path at the edge of the forest. "That way."

Chapter 22

Twenty minutes later, they were attacked by a band of ten giant rats carrying swords and wearing leather armor. Their energy weapons destroyed the rats without any difficulty.

Time seemed to flow much the same in this universe as in their own. The hours marched on into evening. Before night could fall, they came to a stockade made of pointed tree trunks fixed upright into the ground. Human soldiers in cloaks and metal chest plates patrolled the top of the stockade. One of them looked down at them without much interest, pointed to the left and said, "Gate's that way."

"Thanks," Michael said. The soldier nodded.

A few minutes later, they came to a gate in the stockade with a soldier standing guard on either side of it. One raised a brow at Michael and his little party and appeared to examine their armor with a critical eye. The other said, "Business?"

"We'd like dinner and a room for the night." The soldiers shared a look. The second one nodded. The first pointed through the gate. "Down the street; turn left, then another right. They'll take care of you."

They walked through the gate, the soldiers giving them speculative looks, and followed the directions they had been given. They walked down a paved road and soon came to a large three story log building with a sign over the front entrance that said, 'Wayfarers' Inn.' They walked up the steps to a neatly laid out deck with a log swing flanked by two wooden seats, and walked through the front door into a lobby. A fireplace with logs burning merrily away, a rug and three padded leather chairs hugged the wall to their left. A long wooden counter stood to the right. As they walked in, a bored looking clerk with a bald head looked up and gave them a surprised smile. "Can I help you?"

"We'd like some dinner and rooms for the night? Four rooms, if you have them." Michael had no idea what these people would make of Romulus. They had agreed that he would wait for them in the woods.

The clerk smiled wider. "Of course, sir." He tapped the keys of an ancient looking but functional computer and handed them four keys and a sheet of paper. "Your receipt. The dining room is at the end of the hall. Elevator straight ahead."

They looked at each other. Curly shrugged. Gloriosa looked bewildered. "Thanks," Michael said.

The clerk smiled and looked back down at his screen.

Despite the log exterior, the inside of the building was climate controlled and comfortable. The floor was polished wood. The lights were fluorescent. The elevator carried them up to their rooms, all in a row on the third floor. Each room had a bathroom with hot and cold water, a sink and a shower. The beds were large, with foam mattresses over wooden frames. All very civilized.

They met in the dining room twenty minutes later and were greeted by a hostess wearing a black skirt and a white blouse, her blonde hair held back by a pink, plastic hairband. "Table for five?"

"Yes," Michael said. "Thank you."

She gave them a wide smile. "This way," she led them to a large table beneath a window. Four other tables were occupied, two with couples, one with a man, a woman and three young children. The last held a man sitting alone, dressed in a cloak. A wooden staff leaned against the table and a floppy, cloth hat sat on another chair. He was just finishing up his meal. He patted his lips with a napkin, picked up his hat and the staff and walked over to their table. "Welcome," he said. "We don't get a lot of you folks here, anymore. It's a pleasure to see that we haven't been forgotten. You'll be wanting the castle. Turn right when you get out of the gate and just follow the road. Shouldn't be much trouble for you, not dressed like that. Excellent looking armor. Good luck."

They stared at him. "Uh, thanks," Michael said.

He gave them a wide grin, tipped his hat and walked out, staff gently thumping on the floor.

Richard Norlin frowned down at the table. Curly and Rosanna gave each other questioning looks. "I don't understand this," Gloriosa said.

Neither did Michael. "I guess we'll find out tomorrow," Michael said. "At the castle."

They were attacked twice more, once by another, larger band of the mutated rats, once by a flock of eagles with three meter wingspans. Neither the rats' claws nor the eagles' talons could pierce their armor and the attacks were easily repelled. After two hours hiking through shady woods, they exited the forest into a large field covered with short, green grass. Sheep grazed placidly in the meadow.

In the distance, a stone castle, with white spires shining in the sun, rose toward the sky. A few minutes more brought them to the front gate, made of thick wooden planks held together with iron bands. The gate opened. A butler, short, bald and stout, gave them a reserved smile. "Welcome to Briarwood Keep. Please come in."

Five minutes later, they were sipping sherry from cut crystal glasses and looking out upon the meadow and the woods beyond through a floor to ceiling window. Bookcases filled with leather bound volumes covered the three remaining walls of the spacious room. The butler had conducted them to an elevator, which rose to the castle's highest level, shown them to the library and then withdrawn.

A minute later, the door opened and a tall, thin man with hollow cheeks, a high, arched nose, dressed like a Regency dandy, with lace ruffles at his wrists and neck and leather boots covering his calves, walked in, smiled and sat down. "So," he said. "What can we do for you?"

Richard Norlin, Michael noted, was smiling. The others looked bewildered. "Who are you?" Michael asked. "And what is this place?"

"Ah." The tall man cocked his head to the side. "Would I be correct in assuming that you are not gameplayers?"

"No," Michael said carefully. "We're not."

The tall man sat down, picked up the decanter of sherry, poured himself a glass and sipped. "My name is Wendell Halliday," he said, then he grinned. "At the moment, I am Lord Amberley, Master of Briarwood Keep."

"At the moment?"

Wendell Halliday nodded. "I used to be an accountant. Then I ran for the office of County Executive, a position that I still hold.

You might say that Lord of Amberley is an honorary title. Frankly, this is the first time I've been asked to assume the role."

"I'm confused," Michael said.

"Tell me who you are and why you're here. Perhaps I can enlighten you."

Michael glanced at his comrades, none of whom seemed inclined to speak. "To put it simply, our ship was grabbed by a tractor beam and is currently being held in an installation on Chronos. We didn't know what else to do so we tried to explore the installation and discovered three gateways into what appeared to be pocket universes. Here we are." Michael shrugged.

Wendell Halliday raised an eyebrow. "I see." He drained his glass of sherry, poured himself another and sat back in his chair. "Well, every few years, we go back to service the 'installation,' as you call it. The tractor beam was originally put in to prevent landing mishaps." He frowned. "Events on the other side of the gate don't have a lot of interest for us, not since the Empire's fall. This"—he waved a hand—"is part of what was originally intended to be an amusement park."

Richard's grin and quiet little nod told them that he had already figured this out. Wendell Halliday smiled. "It has stood, with very little change, for over two thousand years, as the Empire reckoned time." He grinned. "Considerably longer by our time. People would pay good money to go on a quest, to rescue a princess from an orc or a troll, to wander around in the wilderness and conquer strange creatures and exotic enemies. Our own people use it as well, of course. The place has waxed and waned in popularity over the years but in the end, we've always felt that it deserved to be preserved, as an historical curiosity if nothing else.

"We were alerted when you came through the gate, and as you say, here you are." He raised an eyebrow. "Except for your robot companion. It wasn't necessary for you to hide him, but I can understand your caution."

"An amusement park," Michael said.

Wendell Halliday nodded. "Thousands of years ago, at the dawn of the space age, there were a number of speculative novels that used the theme of artificial worlds set up in pocket universes—alternate dimensions, they were sometimes called—usually by some godly and long forgotten intelligence. The protagonists of these stories were always subjected to various trials and tribulations before being allowed to return home. *Through the Looking Glass, The Chronicles of Narnia, The World of Tiers*…there were many others, and there were even earlier variations from the pre-scientific age, such as Hercules' sojourn in Hades, the Norse myth of Valhalla or the Christian legends of Heaven and Hell." Wendell Halliday grinned. "I think that it must have pleased the builders very much to construct such an obvious entertainment as an amusement park on the other side of the gate. They called the place, appropriately enough, Wonderland."

"What else is here," Michael said, "aside from this amusement park?"

"It's a small universe, barely five light years across. There is only one sun and one habitable planet. We have no star ships because there are no stars, though I know that the information needed to construct them still resides in the databases. Aside from the park, there were originally a few small cities on this side of the barrier, which have grown tremendously in the years since the fall. It's a civilized world that we live in but it's only one world.

"The Empire fell. There was war and then revolution. The outside Universe seemed a bleak and dangerous place. Our leaders have often discussed trying to re-engage with it but the risks never seemed to outweigh the benefits." Wendell Halliday gave a hesitant smile. "And now, the Universe has re-engaged with us."

"The rats?" Michael said. "The enormous bull? The giant eagles?"

Wendell Halliday waved his hand. "Organic robots, all part of the scenario. People enjoy pretending to slay them." He smiled. "You haven't encountered the dragons. Just as well, I suppose.

"We weren't sure who you were or what you were expecting when you came through the gate, and your armor does look functional, though rather exotic. It seemed better to play along."

"And you were an accountant and are now County Executive."

Wendell Halliday tipped his glass toward Michael. "Death and taxes. There's always work for another accountant."

Chapter 23

They spent a week exploring Chronos Two. As Wendell Halliday had said, it was a civilized world. It was also a very old world. The seas were shallow and laden with salt. The mountains, what was left of them, had eroded over the millennia to gentle swells. Tectonic activity had long since ceased.

The zoos were interesting. Native life had evolved no further than the protozoa stage, before the First Empire had moved in and terraformed the planet. Still, evolution had done its work and though the ancestry of the animals in their zoos and nature preserves could be vaguely determined, most of them bore little outward resemblance to their Earthly cousins.

Everywhere they went, armed guards accompanied them. The crowds were orderly but the looks they received seemed less than friendly. Once, an elderly man threw a rock at them as they were conducted down a city street. The guards quickly shoved him away as he shouted something unintelligible. Michael cast a quizzical look at Romulus, who had joined them after their brief sojourn at Brierly Keep. Romulus shook his head.

That evening, at dinner, Wendell Halliday explained. "This Universe is much smaller than the one that our ancestors came from. Gravitational time dilation entails a direct ratio between the amount of mass and energy and the relative rate at which time passes. The ratio is approximately fifty to one. A few hours outside might be many days to us. We're not aware of this, of course. To us, time passes as it always has. But you will find, when you return to your own Universe, that only a few hours have gone by. The First Empire mastered the secrets of creating a new cosmos but they had no power to change the natural laws that exist in this time and space." He shook his head, troubled. "By the time our ancestors settled on this world, it had already aged well beyond the age of old Earth. Our sun is much further along on its natural sequence. In less than fifty thousand years of our time, it will expand into a red giant, engulfing this planet."

They were sitting in a private dining room in a very elegant restaurant on the fifty-seventh story of a building in the capital city of Donnelly, named for Estelle Donnelly, director of the original project that had led to the creation of this pocket universe. The city of Donnelly was situated on the edge of a sea, nearly fifteen hundred kilometers from Wonderland.

Wendell Halliday seemed to have taken it upon himself to be their tour guide, or perhaps he had been appointed to do so. He didn't say and they didn't ask.

Far below them, streetlights shone, faintly outlining pedestrians. There were no roads in this part of the city. All the traffic flew through the air. It must have been computerized, Michael thought. Otherwise, there would have been chaos. Instead, softly shining globes flicked smoothly past each other outside their window.

Michael kept his face impassive through the excellent meal but it was clear that there was trouble in paradise. For one thing, they had been kept away from the crowds. The holos had mentioned them. The news sites contained the information that visitors from the old Universe had arrived on their fair world...but that was all. Few details were given. And then there were the plainclothesmen, four hard eyed men and women, standing guard in the four corners of the room. Wendell Halliday had shown them to a large private suite on the rooftop of Donnelly's most exclusive hotel and left them alone for the night. Otherwise, he rarely left their side.

Michael fingered a cut crystal wine glass. The meal had been delicious, one course following another, mostly vegetables, a small portion of fish, a tiny cube of some exquisite, marinated meat, and a dessert of a caramelized fruit stuffed with a sweetened liqueur and encased in a chocolate crust.

The wait staff had said not a word, efficiently placing the plates in front of them and then whisking them away when they were empty.

An old world, Michael thought. A doomed world. Not right away, of course. Fifty thousand years in the future seemed hardly worth worrying about, but still...Wendell Halliday's face was grim.

"What's troubling you?" Curly asked.

Michael had learned that Curly, despite his appearance, was both perceptive and thoughtful. The question did not surprise him, though it appeared to surprise Wendell Halliday, who sat back in his seat, fingered his wineglass and sighed. "It is said that the realization of death helps wonderfully to concentrate the mind. We live long. Many of our citizens have lived for over a thousand years. Our ancestors escaped the holocaust on Electra and came here, to a new world."

Halliday's eyes skittered across the guards, silently standing at their posts, and down onto the street below. "This is a prosperous, peaceful world, but not so peaceful as it used to be. Strange things happen to a people when they lose hope for the future. Some revel in orgies of sex and drugs. Some become depressed. Some of these stop eating and fade away, or simply walk off a cliff or even shoot themselves in the head. Others go about their lives, grimly determined to do their best. Some few dedicate themselves to escaping the tragedy. And some devote themselves to cults and superstitions. We are beginning to see the early stages of all of these."

"The larger Universe is still out there," Michael said. "Fifty thousand years is a long time. You can escape."

"Can we? Think about it. Chronos is a lifeless, airless moon. We could go through the gateway, but then what? There is nothing to sustain us."

"You need ships," Rosanna said. "You can go down to Electra. In fifty thousand years, the radiation will have faded away. It will be an Earth like world by then, just as it was before."

"Ah, but you forget about the time dilation. Fifty thousand years to us, will be only a thousand or so years to Electra. No, our home planet will still be a radioactive wasteland."

Rosanna shrugged. "There are billions of other stars in the galaxy, with billions of planets."

"Yes, this is true," Halliday said. "You are of course correct. We need ships. With ships, we can escape, and in the end, we will build them. We will have no choice, not if we wish to survive. We shall do so. We *must* do so, but it is remarkable how much denial human beings are capable of, how so many can refuse to see what is right in front of their faces. Some…" Halliday shrugged. "They just won't admit that it's going to happen. They're hoping for a miracle."

"You have fifty thousand years to convince them," Michael said.

"Why the guards?" Richard Norlin said. Gloriosa, evidently thinking along the same lines as Richard, silently nodded.

"Because we may not have fifty thousand years to convince them." Halliday grimaced and poured himself a large glass of brandy from a decanter. "You see, it is not only the sun and the planet that is aging. The Universe itself is aging."

Richard nodded. Curly looked thoughtful.

Wendell Halliday sipped his brandy. "There are many theories regarding the ultimate fate of the Universe. One theory holds that expansion is infinite. According to this theory, the Universe will descend into eternal cold and darkness, when the very last sun has exhausted its fuel and burned itself out. Another theory says that the Universe will contract into a singularity, perhaps presaging another Big Bang and the birth of a new Universe. One theory says that as expansion reaches a certain point, the density of the Universe will decrease until it reaches some critical threshold, and all matter will then be ripped apart into its component particles.

"As I said, this Universe has aged very rapidly..." He sighed. "According to our observations of this admittedly limited Cosmos, the density of space is indeed decreasing."

"Oh," Michael said.

"So, you see, we may not have fifty thousand years." Halliday grinned sadly. "We may not have fifty years."

"Their population totals nearly seven billion," Romulus said. "In order to evacuate seven billion people, they will need approximately one million very large ships."

"Not if they put them in cold sleep," Michael said. "A few thousand ships would do."

"With seven billion containment tanks," Curly said. "Still, a very large undertaking."

"Or," Michael said. "They could decide to upload their minds. That would require only one ship plus the necessary memory cores."

Richard and Gloriosa, from a less scientifically advanced culture, looked bewildered at this. Curly and Rosanna both winced. "Most of the populace here regards mind uploading as an unsatisfactory course of action," Romulus said. "In their opinion, this would make copies of their minds but would not save their lives. It is the least popular of the possible solutions."

The dinner had ended soon after Wendell Halliday's pronouncement. They had retreated to their suite, accompanied to the door by their very watchful guards.

"There is much that Wendell Halliday did not say," Romulus said. "I have been monitoring their transmissions. Civil unrest has been growing. There have been acts of sabotage, ostensibly random but probably coordinated."

They sat together in the living room of their suite, peering out at the darkness. The night was clear but the absence of stars seemed somehow both ominous and insubstantial. The furniture was solid and well made, their surroundings comfortable...but after their discussion at dinner, it all seemed very fragile, very...temporary.

This is not our problem, Michael thought. "There is nothing we can do to help them." They all looked at him. He blinked, startled. He hadn't realized that he had spoken out loud.

"No," Romulus said. "Not really. Even if we left this instant, returned to the Empire and sought assistance, it would be at least a century of Chronos time before that assistance could arrive, even assuming that the Empire was willing to provide it. I do not think that even the First Empire could have marshalled a million ships, or seven billion containment tanks and enough ships to hold them all. Not in time to do these people any good."

"We should leave," Gloriosa said.

"Before it's too late," Richard added.

They were right. This world's fate was in its own hands. "We'll speak to our hosts in the morning," Michael said.

Their schedule for the next day included a visit to Government Center. The Prime Minister and various members of her party wished to meet them. After much debate, it had been decided that the government would gain more benefit from publicizing their existence than by keeping it a secret. Michael and his crew were not consulted on this decision.

They left the hotel in a glowing, golden sphere with soft comfortable seats and no driver. "The pods are completely automated," Wendell Halliday said. "Sit back and relax. Would any of you like some music? No?" he shrugged. "You can blank out the view if heights make you uncomfortable."

Heights did not make Michael uncomfortable. Being crowded into a small pod with no control over their destination and no way to escape did. The others seemed to feel the same way. Their expressions were uneasy.

Wendell Halliday gave them a tentative smile. "There will be cameras, and reporters. No doubt they will ask you questions. Ignore them if you wish. Speak to them if you would like. The government has nothing to hide. You'll be given a prominent place in the visitors' gallery. We want you to be seen."

"Being seen is all very well," Michael said, "and within limits, we're happy to cooperate, but we have business of our own, on the other side of the barrier. We appreciate the hospitality that you've shown us, but we would like to be on our way."

Wendell Halliday nodded. "I understand. We were expecting as much, particularly after our conversation yesterday evening. Would tomorrow be acceptable?"

They were, in fact, entirely at their hosts' mercy. Curly and Rosanna looked at each other. Gloriosa shrugged. Richard Norlin appeared unhappy. "Yes," Michael said. "Tomorrow would be quite acceptable."

If they meant it. Michael thought that they did. Wendell Halliday at least seemed sincere, but then, the stock in trade of all good politicians, like all good con men, was the ability to fake sincerity.

Their trip passed uneventfully. The sun shone brightly in a bright, blue sky. Far in the distance, the sea could be seen, its waters placid. The city beneath their pod appeared clean and orderly. Fifteen minutes after they took off, the pod descended to a small landing field, where a platoon of guards met them. A railing surrounded the field, and on the other side of the railing, a crowd pressed inward. They were screaming, a jumble of noise. Very little of it was pleasant, most of it consisting of admonitions to go back where they came from.

Michael agreed wholeheartedly.

One man, tall, fat and poorly dressed, could be clearly heard. "Empire bastards. Filthy Empire bastard! Get off our world!"

"They seem rather vehement," Richard said.

"Ignore them," Wendell Halliday said. "They represent only one faction. Very few share their bigotries."

They headed for the gate, surrounded by their guards. The gate opened into the first floor of Government House. Inside, they stood beneath a marble rotunda, capped by a dome perhaps thirty meters high. Here, the crowd was quiet. A tall woman with black hair, dark skin and dark blue eyes waited for them, standing on the first level of a row of curved steps. She was smiling. "Prime Minister Sheila Atkins," Wendell Halliday said.

A man stood on either side of the Prime Minister, one tall, white haired and stooped, the other short, black haired and apparently much younger. Both had similar, eager expressions on their faces. "Cultural Minister Brett Lane and Minister of the Interior, Quentin Davis," Wendell Halliday said. A line of troops surrounded these three. Set a meter or so back, a red velvet rope hung between upright metal posts and beyond the rope stood an orderly crowd, all with recorders hovering over their shoulders.

Wendell Halliday nudged Michael and they all began to walk. As they neared, the Prime Minister stepped down. She was a very tall woman, almost as tall as Michael. "Welcome," she said. "I hope that you've been enjoying your stay."

Michael nodded. "Thank you. It's been very pleasant."

A few clichés regarding the universal solidarity of mankind, a rumination on their hopes for the future and a brief statement of thanks followed, then they all marched in to an enormous amphitheater. The journalists, or so they appeared to be, trooped in with them. So far, nobody but the Prime Minister had said a word to them. As they walked, she leaned over to Michael and whispered. "We've arranged a short press conference for after the session. I hope you don't mind."

Would it do any good if they did? Michael smiled. "Of course not," he said. "Anything we can do to help."

The Prime Minister smiled and patted his arm. She glanced at Wendell Halliday, then back to Michael. "I hope to speak with you later. I understand that you're anxious to return to your own world." And apparently, their pod had been bugged. Michael was not surprised.

"Of course. We're at your disposal."

Michael and the crew were given seats mid-way up in a private booth on the second level, where they were prominently displayed, both to the surrounding crowd and the assembled dignitaries below.

The debate that followed was about what Michael had expected. One side, the Prime Minister's side, wanted to build ships as quickly as possible and evacuate. Another, arguing against the cost, wanted to upload all of their minds, an obviously cheaper and faster alternative. A third advocated sitting tight. The evidence that their Universe was about to annihilate itself was, after all, sparse and largely theoretical. From the murmurs of the crowd, this position seemed to have considerable support. Yet another, not quite identical to but supporting the third, represented by a slim man wearing a clerical collar, argued that the Lord's divine plan marched inevitably onward, and that they should stay and play out their appointed role. "The soul is infinite," this man said. "If the material Universe vanishes, then our souls will remain, transmuted into the care of our Heavenly Father." Most of the crowd seemed unconvinced by this statement but listened politely, nonetheless.

Michael and the crew figured prominently in the debate. "We must thank our unexpected visitors," the Prime Minister said. "For the first time in many thousands of years, we have been given real knowledge of the outside Universe. The Empire that our ancestors knew has fallen but a new Empire has arisen. Humanity inhabits thousands of worlds. There is a place for us in that Universe…"

Maybe. Seven billion people was a lot of people. You couldn't just dump them on some empty world. Most of them would starve to death within a week Where would you put them? How would you house them and feed them? No, unless some sort of arrangements were made, and it was hard to imagine what those arrangements might be, they would become a wandering fleet, dropping a few hundred here, a few hundred there. It would take decades to find places for them all. They would live but they would be a scattered people. They would lose whatever remained of their history and their culture.

Gloriosa rose to her feet and quietly stepped to the aisle, presumably heading to the rest rooms. Two guards accompanied her.

The debate went on. The same points were re-hashed over and over. Michael glanced at his interface. Gloriosa should have returned by now.

A scream erupted from the back of the amphitheater. The crowd turned, stared. A woman staggered into the aisle. "They're dead," she cried. "They've been murdered!" She swayed, gasping, and then her eyes rolled back in her head and she collapsed.

Chapter 24

"We'll find her," Wendell Halliday said, his voice subdued. He sounded as if he were trying to reassure himself more than Michael.

The two guards were indeed dead, their bodies stuffed into stalls in the ladies' room. They had been shot with lasers, which cauterized the wounds and left very little blood. They had also been stabbed multiple times each, which left quite a lot of blood, indeed. Whoever did it had planned well. Paper coveralls and shoe covers, dripping with red, were left in the trash bin.

"If she's alive," Michael said.

Wendell Halliday grimly nodded.

Forensics techs swarmed over the room. A tall, hard-eyed woman named Clarice Sullivan was in charge. She had introduced herself to Michael as Donnelly's Chief of Security. She stood at the back of the room, consulting a handheld device, occasionally speaking into it in a low whisper. There must have been a security screen around her since Michael could see her lips moving but couldn't hear a sound. He could read lips, however. Perhaps best not to let them know that.

So far, he had suspicions but no evidence that their hosts might be responsible. The Prime Minister had given her condolences. Her face was white. Her voice quavered. She seemed sincere. The press conference was not mentioned, presumably canceled for the duration.

"They walked down a back staircase," Clarice Sullivan said. "They avoided people but made no attempt to evade the security cams. A pod was waiting around the side of the building. There were four of them, three men and a woman. They bundled your crewmember inside and took off." She hesitated. "She appeared to be sedated but was alive."

Richard, Curly and Rosanna were hanging back while Michael dealt with the authorities. He could see them quietly speaking among themselves. Romulus, at the request of their hosts, had stayed behind in the hotel. They had wanted the cameras to focus on the people and the Parliamentary debate. Romulus would distract from that.

"What now?" Michael asked.

Clarice Sullivan shrugged. "Their pod has been tracked. They can't hide."

"Who are they? Do you know?"

"Yes. They're a well-known group of radical morons. They've been insisting that the crisis we are faced with is a fraud promulgated by the government. They claim to have evidence that once the majority of the population has evacuated, then the few wealthy who stay behind will steal everything that's left. They're insane."

"Evidence, huh?"

Clarice Sullivan shrugged. "Their so-called evidence consists of nothing more than a few oblique, cynical comments from people far removed from the government. Their theory is nothing more than a wishful fantasy." The corner of Clarice Sullivan's lip twitched upward. "Unfortunately, one of these idiots is William Atkins, the Prime Minister's grandson."

"Awkward," Michael said.

Clarice Sullivan nodded.

"I sympathize with the Prime Minister's situation but I don't really give a damn," Michael said. "I want my crew back."

"The pod is being tracked. When it lands, we'll know."

The pod drifted over the city and came down near a large house surrounded by a high brick wall. During the next hour, seven young men drove into the compound. The door to the mansion opened. The men trooped inside. The door closed. By now, the air over the compound was filled with drones, those of Security, the press and any private citizen who happened to be curious, which was many. A force field covered the compound. The drones could see inside but they couldn't get too close. Clarice Sullivan waited for another hour but there was no further activity in the compound. She had hoped that the attackers might make contact with the authorities. When they did not, she called them.

A face filled the screen, male, young, good-looking, with black hair and striking blue eyes. A webcast displayed the available information to the grid on Michael's retina. Clarice Sullivan presumably had a similar implant. She stood alone in front of the screen.

This wasn't Michael's show. He sat in a chair, off to the side, grateful that he had been allowed to observe.

Giorgio Silva: twenty-seven years old, arrested three times in his late teens for assault. All charges dropped. He inherited a personal fortune of over three million credits from an aunt who died without issue. He is otherwise unemployed.

Michael had no idea what three million of the local credits might translate to. Presumably a lot.

"What are your demands," Clarice Sullivan said.

Giorgio Silva grinned. "I think you already know them."

"Again?" Clarice Sullivan narrowed her eyes. "You're out of your mind. You know that, don't you? Before, it was just games. Now, you've murdered two people and you've taken a hostage. Do you really think that you're in control of this situation?"

"We are if you want your hostage back." Giorgio Silva's eyes gleamed. "And it was never just games."

"We do want our hostage back. She is a citizen of the Second Interstellar Empire of Mankind. Also, she is our guest. She has nothing to do with your ridiculous claims."

Gloriosa was not exactly a citizen of the Second Interstellar Empire, nor was Michael. No point in pointing out these perhaps inconvenient facts, not at the moment. Perhaps later...

"No," Giorgio Silva said, "but then as your guest, and as a citizen of this Second Interstellar Empire, she presumably has value, both to you and to them. So, let us negotiate."

"Fine," Clarice Sullivan said. "You go first. Tell us what you want."

Michael had participated in more than one hostage negotiation. To be successful, you had to establish a little empathy and rapport. Try to convince the hostage takers that you had some sympathy for their position, that if things were just a bit different, you might almost be on their side. Once that connection has been established, maybe you can get them to change their behavior, or at least see reason. Michael had some doubts regarding Clarice Sullivan's technique, but then, in this very old, very ordered society, she probably didn't get a lot of practice.

Giorgio Silva looked annoyed. "It's very simple. The government must drop its plans for this absurd evacuation. The rights of the people must be respected."

Clarice Sullivan nodded. "And in return, what?"

"We will release the hostage, of course."

Clarice Sullivan looked incredulous. "And will you then surrender yourselves to the authorities and answer for your crimes?"

"Do you think we're idiots?" Giorgio Silva asked. "We would be insane to submit ourselves to your so-called justice."

Idiots or insane…that did sort of set the parameters. Definitely, one or the other.

"Do I take that as a 'No?'" Clarice said.

"*Those who doeth evil hateth the light.* It's a very old quote. Have you noticed the drones floating over this compound?" Giorgio Silva said. "We regret the loss of life but it was unavoidable. Your guards died in the service of a tyrannical government. We're not the ones who will have to answer for it."

"So, it's a 'No.'"

"Yes," Giorgio Silva said. "It's a 'No.'"

"Very well," Clarice Sullivan said. "I'll get back to you." She pressed a button. The image in the screen vanished. She sighed and gave Michael a weak grin. "I suppose that could have gone better."

Michael nodded. "Probably."

"I'll have to consult with the Prime Minister."

Not a lot of options here, Michael thought, and the bad guys were probably not the most patient. "Don't take too long."

"No," she said, and hurried off.

The conference room was crowded, mostly with administrators whose bewilderment shone from their faces. Michael had been asked to sit in, for which he was initially surprised but grateful. When he expressed puzzlement at the invitation, Clarice Sullivan smiled. "Our databases are excellent and go back for many thousands of years. We know who you are," she said.

"Ah…"

"Your advice will be helpful, and besides, the outcome affects your crew member."

Indeed, it did. "Certainly," he said. "I'll be happy to participate."

But in the end, he had little to add beyond the obvious, obvious to him, at least. They spoke for over an hour, first Clarice Sullivan, then the Interior Minister, then a supposed expert on criminal behavior, whose expertise was almost entirely theoretical since this society had almost no criminal behavior. The Prime Minister sat in grim silence, wringing a piece of cloth in her hands, her face white. Finally, when the conversation had ground to a halt, Michael spoke up. "You're not going to cancel your evacuation plans. If your calculations are correct, it would mean the death of billions of your citizens. You could offer to forgive their crimes in return for them freeing the hostage. They would probably reject the offer, but are you willing to make it?"

"No," the Prime Minister said.

"I didn't think so." Michael shrugged. "Then you have nothing else to offer."

The death penalty was unknown here. Even jail was considered barbaric. Beyond monetary fines, the only punishment in this society for atavistic or anti-social behavior was implantation with a control drode, as humane a punishment as was humanly possible.

"So then," Michael said, "since you have nothing else to offer, what is your next step?"

Clarice Sullivan frowned. The Interior Minister looked angry but had nothing to say. The Prime Minister stared down at the cloth in her hands.

"Nothing?" Michael sighed. "Then let me clarify things. You have three choices. Wait. Do nothing. Perhaps they will tire of the situation, or perhaps they will try to force the outcome and kill my crew member. Second, give them an opportunity to surrender, which they will most likely refuse, and then storm the compound when they do so, or, third, simply storm the compound.

"Remember, these people are fanatics. Fanatics are not known for their ability to reason."

Four large Security pods floated over the city. The first three pods contained twenty Security officers. The fourth contained nineteen plus Michael. He hadn't needed to ask. They had invited him. At first, the request bewildered him but it wasn't hard to figure out. These people had no enemies. They were alone in their

Universe. Therefore, they had no military. They had a Security Force, whose daily job most often consisted of dealing with minor disputes and white-collar crime, little of it violent.

They weren't used to this. Michael was.

Curly, Rosanna and even Richard had wanted to come along. Michael had reluctantly refused. "You're all good at hand-to-hand and you're good with weapons, but you haven't been trained to work as part of a larger team. We'll have to rectify that, but we can't do it now."

And so here he was, déjà vu all over again. It had been many years since he had participated in an armored assault but it all felt sadly familiar.

The head of the expedition was named Roderick Bailey, a tall, well-built man with graying hair. He had the rank of Colonel. Bailey gave Michael a hard-eyed stare and said, "Stick close to me."

Michael nodded. Both of them knew what Bailey was requesting: *tell me what to do.* It might have been smarter for them to simply put Michael in charge of the operation but despite his unique experience, he didn't know the people, he didn't know the equipment and he didn't know the terrain. Better to keep him in an advisory role.

The equipment was good, however, as good as any Michael had ever worked with. The armor was heavy but it didn't feel heavy, faultlessly augmenting his every movement. The rifle, accurate at long distances, could shoot either bullets or tranquilizing darts. The handgun used a magnetic field to propel explosive pellets. They had even issued him a truncheon and a good old fashioned billy club. They may or may not have known about the plastic knife in a sheath in his forearm. If so, they were too polite to mention it.

The plan was also a good one. It was simple, for one thing. In combat, simple is always best. Hit their screens with lasers and plasma shells. When the screens go down, attack. Rescue the hostage. Capture the bad guys if possible. If not, well, those were the breaks and nobody was going to cry for them except possibly their mothers.

Michael was grimly aware, however, that no plan survives contact with the enemy and this plan had some big question marks. They didn't know how many people were in the mansion. They didn't know how fervently those people might resist. They didn't know what sort of weapons they might have. The bad guys were dilettantes playing at Revolution but they were also fanatics. They might surrender quickly once the violence got real. They might fight to the bitter end. They might blow the place up with all of them inside. It was possible that they themselves didn't know what they would do. Still, if the forces of justice wanted to rescue Gloriosa, they didn't have much choice.

They didn't try to hide and they didn't try to pretend. They ignored the flock of drones. Let the world see what was about to transpire. The Prime Minister had insisted on it and Michael agreed. Their assault pods spread out, one on each side of the mansion. The screen crackled below them as random insects and particles of dust impacted.

"Fire," the Colonel said.

From each pod, a bright green light and glowing tracer shells erupted and splashed against the force field. The field resisted for a moment, then it flared and went down in an eruption of sparks.

"Go," the Colonel said.

The pods swooped down, landed, one on each side of the house and split open. Michael's pod landed in the front, as close as they could get it to the tall, wooden door. Wide, plexiglass windows stood on each side of the door. They had all reviewed the layout. One window opened into a den, the second into a private office.

All twenty of them piled out, the Colonel in the lead with Michael at his side. No opposition so far. Two armored troopers unrolled a string of grey putty, stuffed it around the front door, attached two electrical leads that led to a small, metal box and stepped back. They all spread out to the side. The Colonel pressed a button on the box. The putty exploded. The door fell inward.

Five troopers dived through each window, the glass shattering against their armor. Michael threw a concussion grenade through the opened doorway, followed it up with a second grenade that spewed teargas and a third that emitted thick, black smoke. They waited ten seconds.

"Go," the Colonel said again.

Their suits contained an independent oxygen supply and their optics could see in the infra-red. The smoke was not a hindrance. They charged, bullets pinging against their armor. Inside, at least ten young men clustered. Their eyes streamed with tears but they still clutched guns, which they fired randomly through the dark. Michael ignored the bullets. They couldn't get through his armor. Laser fire might, but smoke absorbed the lasers' energy, making them almost useless.

Michael and the others waded in and within moments, all ten of the opposition were disarmed and down on the floor, their arms and legs tied together.

They could hear screams and the sound of sporadic bullets coming from the rest of the house but these soon ceased. An armored trooper came up to them, nodded at Michael and saluted the Colonel. "All secure except the main bedroom. We have a situation."

"Gloriosa?" Michael asked.

"The bedroom."

Michael sighed and the Colonel shook his head. "Let's go see."

The door to the bedroom was unlocked. Inside, Gloriosa sat in a chair, her arms and legs tied together. She was breathing but appeared to be unconscious. Giorgio Silva stood behind the chair, holding a knife against Gloriosa's throat. His nostrils flared. His eyes darted around the room. "You were supposed to negotiate," he said.

Michael's hand rose and his gun spat. A small, black hole appeared in Giorgio Silva's head. The head went *poof* and disappeared in a spray of bone and blood. The knife fell from his hand and Giorgio Silva's suddenly headless body slid to the floor.

"Sorry to disappoint you," Michael said.

The Prime Minister's grandson turned out to be one of the young men tied up in the den. He was marched out with all the rest. Three of these had suffered broken bones in the fight. Two had concussions. Giorgio Silva was the only fatality. Gloriosa was quickly checked out by medics at the scene. "They've sedated her," one of the medics said. He shrugged. "I don't know what they gave her but she's breathing and she should wake up as soon as the stuff wears off." They loaded her onto a stretcher, wrapped her in a blanket and trundled her out the front door.

Sheila Atkins waited for them outside. She and her grandson ignored each other as he was marched past. One-by-one, she thanked the Security officers as they exited the mansion. Michael was the last. As the cameras recorded every moment, she shook his hand and said, "I know that you're anxious to be leaving. Please come by my office tomorrow morning." She smiled sadly. "I have a favor to ask you, and I have someone that I would like you to meet."

"Of course," Michael said. "I'll be looking forward to it."

They returned to the *London* a little before noon the next day. As Wendell Halliday had said, only a few hours had passed in their own Universe. The tractor beams were disengaged. They ran through a systems check, floated out of the installation and watched it vanish behind them. Michael breathed a sigh of relief.

"Well, that was fun," Richard said.

Gloriosa, sitting at the table with a cup of hot tea, gave him a peeved look. Gloriosa had awakened a few hours after her rescue and was able to describe what had happened. As they had surmised, her guards had been murdered by a swarm of young men. Gloriosa had been overpowered and then restrained, though the training Michael had given her enabled her to break the arm of one attacker and the nose of another. They injected her with something. Her head began to swim and she remembered nothing more until she came to in the hospital.

Curly and Rosanna looked at the newest member of their party and appeared a bit embarrassed.

"Think nothing of it," Catherine Halliday said. "I understand."

Catherine Halliday was one-hundred-five years old, though she appeared no older than twenty-five. She was Wendell Halliday's mother. Michael had met her only a few hours before, in Sheila Atkins' office.

"Catherine is one of my oldest friends," the Prime Minister had said. "We went to school together. She served as the Governor of Kilaway Province for twelve years and now spends her time gardening." The Prime Minister gave Catherine Halliday a faintly disapproving smile. Catherine smiled back.

The office contained a wooden desk, a rug over a hard-wood floor, a small coffee table, a couch against one wall, a large window and three comfortable looking chairs. In the distance, the placid sea rippled in the morning light. "Can I offer you anything?" the Prime Minister asked. "Roobios? Tea?"

"No thank you," Michael said. "I've eaten."

The Prime Minister crisply nodded. "So, then, I won't keep you. Briefly, I wanted to thank you once again. My grandson is in police custody but he is alive. He has misbehaved and will be punished, along with his idiotic colleagues, but he is still my grandson." She sighed. "Also, the conspiracy of which he was a part has been discredited. I have a little more room to maneuver than I had before." The Prime Minister glanced at Catherine Halliday. "I am asking you for a favor. Take Catherine with you. Deliver her to your authorities. She will be our ambassador to the Second Interstellar Empire of Mankind."

Michael blinked. The request made sense and he saw no reason to refuse. "Of course," he said. "I would be honored."

The Prime Minister seemed to relax. "Good. We're going to have to build ships. A lot of ships. The legislation has been prepared and will be introduced within the next few days, while we still have the public's sympathy. Nobody will be forced to board those ships. I understand human nature. Many of our people—perhaps most—will refuse to believe in the coming apocalypse. They won't leave." She shrugged. "Still, billions of us will, and we will need a place to go. Catherine's job is to arrange that for us."

Catherine Halliday was a beautiful woman of average height, with a full figure, long, dark hair, smooth unlined skin and a serene face. "Sheila has been trying to convince me for years to get back in the action. Somebody has to do this. It might as well be me." She grinned at Michael and raised an eyebrow. "I also have grandchildren. Our circumstances sometimes change in ways we don't expect but life goes on. I want my children and my grandchildren to live, and I was getting a little bored."

After their time on Baldur and then Kodiak, the *London*'s database was as up to date as possible. Michael queried it before they drifted away from the tiny moon and within a few minutes he had the information he wanted. There were five possibilities, worlds that were civilized, that were members of the Second Empire or at least valued trading partners, worlds that had a solid industrial infrastructure but were, for one reason or another, under-populated…worlds that had room. One in particular intrigued him. He had known this world, two thousand years ago.

"Huh," he said.

The others looked at him. He grinned at Catherine Halliday. "I think I may have found what you're looking for. It's at least a place to start." He turned to Romulus. "Set our course for Illyria."

Chapter 25

"Ambassador Halliday, Captain Glover," Governor Truscott said. "Welcome."

The Governor was short and stout, with bright black eyes and a perpetual smile on his face. Something about him made Michael uncomfortable, though. Maybe it was the excessive enthusiasm. The Governor seemed almost to bounce in his seat as he talked. Hard to say.

The Governor looked at the holograph floating over his desk and gave a brisk nod. "We are always eager to make contact with a new world, of course, particularly one with advanced technology; and Captain Glover—your credentials are impressive, indeed. The contribution you made toward resolving the situation on Kodiak is much appreciated. Captain Lanier speaks most highly of you. However, I'm afraid that I cannot approve your request." His eyes flicked to Catherine Halliday, sitting silently by Michael's side.

Michael blinked. He had expected some hemming and hawing, some guarded uncertainty, possibly a long, boring negotiation. This blanket rejection surprised him. "May I ask why not?" Catherine Halliday asked.

"Because I am only nominally in charge, here. Are you acquainted with the political situation on this world?"

Once, long ago, Illyria was one of the hundred most important worlds in the First Empire. Its population was large and prosperous, its technology advanced, its products valued throughout known space. Illyrian ships were top of the line. Illyrian Universities were famed to the farthest reaches of the Empire for their rigor and quality.

The first colonists to Illyria were selected for genetic traits that the Empire wished to encourage. They were strong and fast, smart and aggressive, designed for survival in difficult environments. The Empire needed soldiers and Illyrian soldiers were the very best.

Michael and his crew had accessed the world wide web as soon as they emerged from slipspace. The local web confirmed what he had seen in the *London*'s database. The people of Illyria had not changed very much in two thousand years. They were as Michael remembered them, physically tough, smart and aggressive. They reveled in competition of all sorts. They liked to play games. The people had not changed but the world had.

Illyria had at first suffered less than most during the Interregnum but like most worlds suddenly cut off from contact with the larger Universe, their technology and their population had regressed, before finally stabilizing and advancing once more. Then, a thousand years ago, an asteroid struck the Eastern continent. The population of the Eastern continent was nearly eradicated. The few survivors left. Nuclear winter decimated the planet. A dark age followed, that lasted centuries.

The Second Empire had made contact with Illyria nearly a hundred years ago. By that time, the Eastern continent had begun to recover. Grasslands and forests, none of the trees very tall yet, covered most of the interior. Animals were migrating back in. The continent was fallow. The Empire decided to occupy it.

The Western continent by this time had a growing, fairly advanced civilization, divided into more than fifty small nations. The people of Illyria were aware of the Empire's occupation of nearly half their planet but were not in a position to object. They lacked the technology and they lacked a United government. Then, nearly fifty years ago, Meridien, perhaps the richest nation on the Western continent, spearheaded a movement toward solidarity. Trading and military alliances were made. A continental congress was established. The first tentative steps toward a world-wide government were taken.

"I was under the impression that you control this continent," Michael said.

The Governor grimaced. "Not at all. Originally, our installation here was a simple naval outpost. Over the years, our presence has grown, but the Imperial Navy controls most of it. Note that I don't say 'owns' most of it. The presence of a thriving native population on the other side of the world has complicated things. In the past few years, the Western governments have asserted hegemony." The Governor smiled ruefully. "In short, they want us to pay rent and they want us to refrain from expanding our own settlements."

The Empire had established several small cities and numerous farming communities, mostly along the coast. The occupants of these cities were former military personnel who had left the service and, rather than accept transport back to the worlds of the Empire, had decided to settle locally. By now, these former military personnel had two generations of descendants, civilians but citizens of the Empire.

"The Imperial outposts have been allowed to establish their own local governments, under the authority of the Governor." Truscott raised an eyebrow. "That would be myself. I am an appointee, and not a native of this world. When my term in office expires, I will be replaced. Please understand that my authority extends only to the civilian towns and cities along the coast of this continent. Most of the land that the Empire occupies is still controlled by the Navy. Jurisdiction over the rest of it is…hazy."

Catherine Halliday frowned at him.

"And so, you see," the Governor said, "that I have no authority to grant permission for up to seven billion refugees to settle here."

"Who does?" Michael asked.

"Admiral Stephen Reynolds is in charge of the Naval contingent. His agreement would be necessary. In addition, if the Continental Congress of the Western Continent agrees with your proposal, there would probably be no further objection. I suggest that you make your way to Meridien and speak with the Secretary General. His name is Douglas Oliver."

It was quickly apparent that a certain level of tension, if not animosity, existed between the Navy and the civilian governments of Illyria. The situation here was certainly unusual, a world divided between Imperial and non-Imperial forces. In Michael's time, many alien (and a few rebellious human) worlds had been occupied by the Empire, but in all those cases, the Empire had ruled, usually with an iron fist. Here, the new Empire's authority extended over a single continent. That authority was divided among military and civilian personnel, and its extent was now being challenged by the representatives of a sizeable native population.

Admiral Reynolds was an old-school bulldog. He wasn't exactly discourteous but he made it plain that he had no time for diplomatic niceties. "The governor told it to you straight," he said. "If this were an Empire world, he and I together could decide things. That's not the case, here. Our occupation of this continent is being disputed in the High Court on Reliance." He shrugged. "No way to tell how that's going to go." He sat back and eyed Catherine Halliday with what might have been disapproval. "Here are my terms…our terms, really, since I've been talking to the Governor and we both agree: the Navy and the civilian authority is going to retain all the territory from the Eastern coast to five hundred kilometers inland. Your people, if they want to settle here, can have the rest of it. In return, you will share your technology with the Empire and you will become Imperial citizens. You can retain your own local administration but otherwise, you will be entirely subject to Imperial governance."

Beggars can't be choosers, Michael thought. This was a good deal. Catherine evidently agreed. "That seems eminently fair," she said.

The Admiral frowned. "Seven billion people? It will be crowded."

Crowded, indeed, but despite his frown, the Admiral did not seem displeased, which made perfect sense, since the presence of an additional seven billion Imperial citizens would certainly bolster their case before the High Court. It was one thing to evacuate a couple of hundred thousand people and a Naval base, if the Illyrians succeeded in their suit. It was quite another to displace seven billion.

"Governor Truscott," Michael said, "has indicated that the native authorities must also agree to this plan. That seems unlikely."

The Admiral grinned. "That's your problem. I've given you our conditions. You're going to have to deal with the native authorities yourselves." The Admiral, obviously, had his doubts. He chuckled. "Good luck."

Chapter 26

Meridien was a small nation that wielded influence out of all proportion to its size. It consisted of a series of islands in the temperate zone of the Western continent plus a few square kilometers on the mainland. The largest island, also the capital city, was named Aphelion. The city had been occupied for over three thousand years and looked much the same as Michael remembered it, more than two millennia ago: towering skyscrapers, clean streets, a busy harbor bustling with ships.

The island of Aphelion was smaller than it had been, however. The sea had risen. The ancient spaceport, on a low-lying island close to the city, was now entirely underwater. A new port had been constructed on another, otherwise barren island. As instructed, the *London* settled gently into its berth.

"Be careful here," Michael said. They were sitting around the large table in the galley, eating breakfast. "These people can be prickly."

Gloriosa picked at her food, seeming to pay the conversation little attention. Her mood had remained glum since her recent abduction. Michael was worried about her. Catherine Halliday gave Gloriosa a concerned look but remained silent.

Curly looked at Michael quizzically. Rosanna smiled and chewed a piece of bacon. "What exactly do you mean?" Richard asked.

"The original colonists were selected for traits that the First Empire considered desirable. They wanted to breed a race of soldiers. The experiment succeeded. Illyrians tend to be...aggressive."

"Is that so?" Curly said.

"They won't attack you without provocation. The laws are strict." Michael frowned. The laws had been strict two thousand years ago. The laws may have changed. "Just be polite."

Curly, Rosanna and Richard exchanged glances. Some wordless communication seemed to take place, which obscurely annoyed Michael. "Yes, Mother," Curly said.

Breakfast over, Romulus tucked securely into his alcove, the rest of them walked down the ship's ramp and found themselves less than a hundred meters from a bright, blue bay. Gulls flew overhead. A light breeze was blowing. Behind them, three small ships in addition to the *London* sat on the tarmac. A ferry boat floated, tied up to a wooden dock. A crewman, his face tanned by the sun, smiled at them. "Going to Aphelion?"

"Yes," Michael said. "Where else do you go?"

"Make the rounds: the city, the mainland, all the larger islands. We knew you arrived during the night, figured you might want transport."

"Thanks." They all trooped aboard and took seats on the outside deck and the ferry smoothly backed away from the dock. Ahead of them, no more than five kilometers away, the buildings and spires of Aphelion rose into the clouds. Pods and flyers swarmed around the buildings. Advertising holograms, fifty meters across and more, flashed in the sky.

"Impressive," Richard said. Gloriosa stared. Curly and Rosanna, by now a bit more used to bright lights and big cities, stared as well. The trip was smooth. The ferry soon docked at a pier that jutted out into the harbor and they walked off through a covered walkway that entered a high, domed terminal, crowded with people.

"Huh," Curly muttered.

Michael suppressed a smile. Curly was staring at the people. Michael had done the same thing on his first visit to Illyria. Michael and Curly were both big men, but they were barely average sized among the citizens of Meridien. Gloriosa looked like a child. She blinked at the people crowding the terminal and the streets outside. "Are they all like this?"

"Pretty much," Michael said.

"Right." Curly shook himself. He turned to Rosanna. "Where to?"

The web here was modern. Directions to any destination in the city were easily accessed.

Rosanna tapped her interface and pointed to the left. "Shops are that way."

Richard shrugged. "Lead on," he said.

"Have fun," Michael said. "I'll see you later."

The four of them trooped off, a determined Rosanna in the lead.

"Ready?" Michael said.

Catherine Halliday nodded. She appeared calm but Michael thought that she was nervous, or perhaps that was only his interpretation of the situation. The fate of her world was riding, almost literally on her shoulders. Michael would have been nervous.

They walked out of the terminal and caught an unmanned pod. Michael programmed the address and a few minutes later they walked into the atrium of a fifty-story building with *Oliver Enterprises* carved into the lintel above the door. A row of receptionists were seated behind a long counter across the middle of the room. A scanner large enough for five people to walk through together stood next to the counter and three large, tough looking men in security uniforms flanked the scanner.

Michael and Catherine walked up to a receptionist, a young woman with straight, blonde hair. "Catherine Halliday and Michael Glover," Catherine said. "We have an appointment with Douglas Oliver."

The receptionist smiled. "Please step through the scanner. Gregory will conduct you."

"I'm carrying weapons," Michael said. "I understood that weapons were permitted."

The guards looked at him. One of them frowned. "Not inside the building. Please leave them here."

Michael carried a small gauss pistol and a knife strapped to his waist. He placed them both in a basket that one of the guards held out. He neglected to mention the plastic knife, supposedly immune to detection, embedded in his forearm.

"Ma'am?" the guard said to Catherine.

She shook her head. "I carry no weapons."

"Then please step through."

No lights, no beeps, no alarms. Michael relaxed. "I'm Gregory," one of the guards said. "Please follow me."

An elevator whisked them smoothly upward to the top floor and opened onto a lobby with a deep, blue carpet, low, comfortable chairs, a coffee table, a sideboard with pastries in a cooling unit, and a coffee dispenser. A security desk with two guards and a second full-body scanner were placed in front of a short corridor. One of the guards consulted a screen. "Catherine Halliday and Michael Glover?"

Both nodded. "Please come through. The door is unlocked. He's waiting for you."

They walked through the second scanner and Michael held the door for Catherine. They stepped into a large office with an expansive view of the harbor and the mainland beyond the water in the distance. Michael barely noticed this. His attention was fixed on the man behind the desk. He was probably average height for a citizen of Illyria, which made him about Michael's size. He was wearing an obviously expensive suit. His shoulders were broad. His hair was auburn, his eyes a deep green. He had a quizzical smile on his face, a smile which grew wider as he stared at Michael. "Michael Glover?"

"And Catherine Halliday," Michael said.

The deep green eyes flicked to Catherine's face. "Of course," he said. "I'm Douglas Oliver. Please sit down."

They sat.

"Can I offer you something?" Douglas Oliver asked. "Coffee? Tea?"

"No thank you," Catherine said. "We've eaten."

"Alright, then. What can I do for you?"

Michael and Catherine had both reviewed all the available information on Douglas Oliver. Fifty years before, he had played a role in ending what had threatened to become a continent-wide war between Gath, a relatively large nation on the West coast and its allies, and Meridien and its allies. The specifics were confusing and hard to find. Somehow, the war had petered out. Gath and Meridien now had excellent relations and Douglas Oliver, at the time an up and coming industrialist, had within twenty years wound up the most powerful man on the continent, first as the Guild Master of Argent, a sort of combination social club, organized crime cartel and investment bank that weirdly formed the government of Meridien, then as the Secretary General of the Continental Congress.

"We sent a preliminary request," Catherine said.

"I've reviewed it. I'd like to hear the details in your own words."

Douglas Oliver listened intently as Catherine spoke. When she had finished, he leaned back in his chair. "So, as many as seven billion refugees may be heading our way. Is that correct?"

Catherine nodded.

"When, exactly, do you expect them?"

She hesitated. "Probably within four months, perhaps a bit sooner."

"How will they know to come here?"

"Before we left Chronos, we identified five likely worlds and determined the order in which we would approach them," Michael said. "Illyria is the first. We transmitted this information back through the gate."

Douglas Oliver nodded, his expression thoughtful. "It won't be seven billion. Some will refuse to leave. How many do you think?"

"Realistically?" Catherine shook her head. "We are a very old people, very set in our ways."

"Time dilation," Douglas Oliver said.

Michael sat up straight. Catherine looked startled. Neither had expected Douglas Oliver to know this. "How old is your civilization, exactly?" he asked.

"Nearly one hundred thousand years."

"Your civilization was derived from that of the First Empire, whose technology was considerably more advanced than any currently in existence." He grinned and cast a glance at Michael. "And then you had an additional one hundred thousand years to develop it further. Is that so?"

"Not entirely." Catherine shook her head. "The population at first was very small and focused on survival. They were fleeing a devastating war on Electra. Many of the refugees had nothing but the clothes on their backs. Food had to be grown, cities built. It took years before we advanced beyond the subsistence level."

Michael listened with half an ear. The story Catherine told was almost universal. Every settled world had its own version.

Catherine shrugged. "Once things settled down, most of us were content to simply live our own lives in our own little Universe. It is true that our databases have access to the technology of the First Empire, and it is true that in some ways our own abilities exceed theirs', but probably not by as much as you would think."

Douglas Oliver nodded. "So, getting back to my prior question, how many of your people do you expect?"

Catherine shook her head. "Most likely considerably less than a billion. I suspect that, in the end, most will refuse to believe that they are in danger."

"They may be right, of course. Theories often turn out to be wrong." He frowned. "Though I suspect that your scientists know what they're doing."

Catherine sat up straighter in her chair. "We cannot force seven billion people to evacuate against their will. It would mean civil war. In that case, none at all would escape."

"So, let me hazard a guess: you regard yourselves as refugees, begging for a handout. Is that correct?"

Catherine sighed. "Of course. Untold millions of people appearing out of nowhere, needing to be housed and fed represents an enormous burden to any government."

"I suspect that you under-rate yourselves. The First Empire could transmute lead into gold. They could create any object out of seemingly thin air, the dream of all the ancient alchemists. We know the theory. E equals mc squared, after all, but in practical terms, the energy requirements are prohibitive."

Catherine Halliday shrugged. "We can build installations within the sun's corona. The available energy there is almost limitless."

Douglas Oliver sat back and nodded. "Excellent," he said. He gave Michael a wolfish smile. "Then let's negotiate."

An interesting man, Douglas Oliver. No doubt he would drive a hard bargain if the circumstances required it, but in this case, his interests and Catherine Halliday's seemed largely the same. The discussion went smoothly. Michael was content to sit and listen.

A code word scrolled across the screen on Michael's retina, a word that only he could see. He blinked. The word repeated. A numbered sequence followed, then a time and a place, and then a query. Douglas Oliver smiled, his eyes flickering to Michael's face. Michael had last seen that code over two thousand years before. He nodded. Douglas Oliver nodded back.

"So," Catherine said, "let me summarize. You will support our petition for sanctuary in return for us becoming citizens of Illyria.

We will share our technology. You will assist in building a sustainable infrastructure on the Eastern Continent."

"Correct," Douglas Oliver said.

"And what will Governor Truscott say to all this? And the naval authorities? I assume that they will also be interested in acquiring our technology, and if we are as valuable as you seem to think, they will presumably prefer that we become citizens of the Empire rather than citizens of your own small world. That, in fact, was one of their conditions for allowing us refuge."

Douglas Oliver smiled. "Every citizen of the Empire is also a citizen of his or her own world. No doubt, the Governor thinks that your presence will bolster the navy's attempts to incorporate Illyria into the Empire. What the Governor does not realize is that, along with our suit against them in the High Court on Reliance, we have also submitted a petition of our own, to become a full-fledged member of the Second Interstellar Empire of Mankind."

Catherine frowned. "I don't understand your politics. What, then, is the issue?"

"Ordinarily, a new world spends a period of time as an Imperial Protectorate. Only after many years is full status granted as an incorporated world, with full voting privileges in the Imperial Senate. During the Protectorate phase, the Governor and the military have close to absolute authority. We have petitioned to bypass Protectorate status."

"Is that ever done?"

"In rare cases, when the new world is sufficiently advanced and if it offers something unique to the Empire."

"Oh," Catherine said.

"Oh, indeed."

Waiting for a ferry every time they wanted transportation to and from the space port did not appeal to any of them, and so Michael had reserved a penthouse suite at The Oliver, a high-rise hotel in the center of Aphelion. Curly, Rosanna, Gloriosa and Richard arrived soon after Michael and Catherine, the men laden with bags and packages, Richard looking bemused, Curly resigned and Rosanna smug. Gloriosa's mood seemed to have lightened. She carried a small box with a new pair of shoes and a large package of chocolates, flavored with the essence of tropical fruits from Illyria's southern islands.

The suite was comfortable, with picture windows looking out at the sea and the space port in the distance, soft carpet and heavy, wooden furniture. Curly, Rosanna and Richard wandered into their rooms. Michael and Catherine settled into a couch and Michael turned on the holoscreen. A sporting event was on the first channel, a martial arts contest. The contestants knew what they were doing and Michael watched the bout and the next two with interest. Catherine sipped from a cup of tea and read a book. Finally, Michael glanced at his interface, turned off the screen and rose to his feet.

Catherine smiled. "What's the story with you and Douglas Oliver?"

"Caught that, did you?" Michael was not surprised. A good politician noticed things. "He seems to know more about me than he should."

"Omega Force? More?"

He gave her a sharp look. "Maybe." He hesitated. "He sent me a coded message, a code that very few people even then had access to, a code that was supposed to be obsolete two thousand years ago. He wants to meet with me—alone."

"When?"

"In twenty minutes."

"The glass is one-way. Nobody can see in," Douglas Oliver said.

They were sitting at a table in a private room on the ground floor of a restaurant called Arcadia. The street outside was clearly visible through the window. The first course, a seafood bisque, had already been served and whisked away. Douglas Oliver was toying with his steak. Michael had three small game birds in front of him. "Is this room clean?" Michael asked.

"Absolutely. I would know."

Michael nodded and picked up one of the birds. Game birds looked elegant on a plate but they were too small to eat with a knife and fork. You had to pick them up with your fingers and nibble on the tiny bones or you wound up throwing away half the meat. "Where did you get the codes?" Michael said. "And how did you know I would respond to them?"

Douglas Oliver grinned. "Damien Oliveros says hello."

Michael went very still, the excellent meal suddenly forgotten. "Damien Oliveros…"

"Dead for over two thousand years…but not forgotten," Douglas Oliver said. He carefully carved a piece of his steak and stolidly chewed it. "Damien Oliveros was my direct ancestor. Some years ago, I was involved in a war. A contingent of mercenary troops under the command of a man who called himself Winston Smith attempted to invade and capture a functioning First Empire installation. In an attempt to halt the invasion, I was given the stored memories of Damien Oliveros. Only a direct descendent could access them, you see." He smiled at Michael. "We succeeded in repelling the invasion but in doing so, the installation was destroyed.

"I am the revenant of Damien Oliveros. I remember you very well. You were Damien Oliveros' friend." He raised an eyebrow. "So, where have you been for the last two thousand years?"

"Sleeping," Michael said.

Douglas Oliver nodded. "And now that you're awake, what do you intend to do?"

Michael licked his fingers and pondered the question. He had been asking himself the same thing. "I'm still considering my options."

"Are you? You've been awake for how long?"

"A few months."

"A few months, and in that time you've been doing…what? Somehow, in only a few months' time, you've managed to acquire an advanced First Empire ship. You have the beginnings of a rather unorthodox crew. You've entered into a retainership with the Imperial navy and you're trying to save seven billion people from annihilation." Douglas Oliver smiled. "It seems to me that you've already found yourself a career, and it's not too different from your prior career."

"I was a soldier," Michael said.

"You were much more than a soldier. You were a soldier who could be counted on."

Michael winced. "What do you want?"

Douglas Oliver leaned forward, his face suddenly intent. "I want your help."

Michael left the restaurant in a daze. The night was warm. The two moons shone overhead. Pedestrians crowded the streets. Aphelion reminded Michael of many other cities. A civilized place, except that the men and women were larger and in better shape than most. Also, the knives and the guns. Everyone seemed to have at least one.

He strolled down the sidewalk, not in a hurry, breathing the fresh air, thinking about the things Douglas Oliver had told him. Two men followed him but kept their distance. They were as well built as all the others on the street but just a trifle smaller. He wasn't exactly surprised but he was disappointed. Did they belong to the Governor or the Admiral? He didn't think they belonged to Douglas Oliver but he couldn't rule it out. He stopped for a moment and peered into a shop window. In the reflection of the glass, he could see the men stop as well. A micro-drone flew out of Michael's pocket, rose into the air and mimicking an insect, flew a meandering path toward the two men. Michael entered the hotel lobby. The two men stopped outside for a moment, conferring, then walked past. The micro-drone followed them.

When he entered the suite, he found Catherine, Richard, Curly and Rosanna sitting around the table, playing poker. Rosanna took two cards from the top of the deck and slid them across. Catherine picked them up and added them to her hand.

"Two credits," Curly said.

"Fold," Richard said. He placed his cards face down on the table.

Gloriosa's tongue peeped out of the corner of her mouth. Her eyes narrowed and she cast a side long glance at Curly. "Raise you one," she said. Gloriosa had trouble getting the hang of the game. No matter how many times the strategy was explained to her, she never dropped out of a hand and always seemed surprised when she lost. This time was no different. Catherine had three jacks. Curly held two pairs. Gloriosa had a single ace. She sat back in her seat and pouted. "I'm going to bed," she announced. "I'm tired of this stupid game."

Richard appeared to be about to say something. Then he thought better of it and cleared his throat. Gloriosa's eyes snapped to his face. "Yes?" she said.

"Nothing," Richard said.

She glared at him, rose to her feet and stalked off.

"I think I've had enough, as well," Rosanna said.

The game broke up a few minutes later and they all drifted off. An hour later, Michael was lying in bed, the lights set to dim, unable to sleep, when a soft knock came at his door. He sat up, pulled on a robe and said, "Come in."

The door opened. Catherine gave him a crooked smile, stepped into the room and closed the door. Michael stared at her. He cleared his throat. "What is it?"

"We haven't talked much since I came on board," she said. "Other than business, that is."

Michael blinked. Catherine was wearing a sheer blouse and a loose, thin skirt. She had changed her clothes since earlier in the evening. "Can't it wait until morning?" Michael asked.

She shrugged. "This seemed like the right time. Can I sit down?"

Michael glanced at the desk chair and nodded.

She smiled at him and sat. "I'm not young any longer," she said. "You know that."

Even in an era when most people lived for nearly half a millennium, a woman's age could be a sensitive topic. He felt it prudent to keep his mouth shut and merely nodded.

"When you live a long time you come to realize that it's almost always wiser to say what you mean. It prevents misunderstandings."

Michael cleared his throat. "So, what do you mean?"

She grinned. "I know that you want me. It's pretty obvious. And you're an attractive man. I don't know how long we'll be together, but for now, there's no reason why we shouldn't indulge ourselves."

Michael looked at her. Catherine projected a sort of calm, knowing aura, profoundly serene. Nothing seemed to surprise her. She dressed simply but her lush figure was never hidden. Michael did want her. He wanted Catherine Halliday as much as any woman he had ever known. He hadn't thought it was obvious, but he wasn't sorry that it was obvious to her. Catherine's lips seemed to glisten in the low light of the desk lamp. "Come here," he said.

She stood up slowly, slipped the blouse off her shoulders, draped it over the back of the chair and walked over to the bed, then she paused and her skirt shimmied to the floor. She wasn't wearing anything underneath it. "I thought you'd say that," she said. "See? No misunderstandings."

Chapter 27

The next morning, he came out of his room, sat down at the table in the lounge and poured himself a cup of coffee. Catherine, already sitting, gave him a soft smile and what might have been the very slightest blush. Gloriosa rolled her eyes. Rosanna grinned. Curly looked bewildered.

"The drone followed them for less than a block and then all contact ceased," Romulus transmitted to his internal server. "During that time, they said nothing but seemed unaware of the drone."

The drone was Second Empire technology. Second Empire agents would no doubt carry portable scramblers.

Douglas Oliver had been under Second Empire scrutiny for years. "They still check up on me, now and then, send a few undercover types around to snoop." He had shrugged, sitting at the table the night before. "I know more about them than I used to. I've had to learn. The war with Gath was a turning point in our relationship with the Empire. They're not as benign as they would like to appear."

Michael frowned at that.

"Do you disagree?"

"No nation, no society, and no individual ever entirely lives up to their own principles. There are always regrettable exceptions, circumstances that are never to be repeated, events outside the norm." Michael shrugged.

Douglas Oliver sniffed. "Go on," he said. "Enlighten me."

Michael grinned. "I haven't been awake for very long. I've formed impressions. Those impressions may not be correct, but my impression is that they try. The Second Empire is considerably more idealistic than the First, at least, they say that they are. They do make it a policy to leave other societies alone."

Douglas Oliver smiled thinly. "Unless those societies have something that they want."

"I don't know," Michael said.

"Winston Smith was willing to kill thousands to gain access to First Empire technology. I have it on excellent authority that he was an agent of his government."

"Was he an agent of his government or was he an agent of an *agency* of his government?"

"That's a thought." Douglas Oliver admitted. "I've had it before." He sat back in his seat, looking glum.

"There are always factions within a bureaucracy, and agencies that feel justified in following their own rules." Michael smiled. "Damien Oliveros knew this very well."

Douglas Oliver morosely nodded. "True."

"And one bureaucracy often has goals that compete with another."

The door opened. The waiter and a busboy entered and began to clear away their empty dishes.

"I've already ordered dessert," Douglas Oliver said. "I think you'll like it."

The waiter placed two small glasses and a bottle on the table. He opened the bottle, poured a small amount of red liquid into Douglas Oliver's glass and waited. Douglas sipped, nodded and said, "Excellent."

The waiter smiled. He and the busboy exited the room.

"Port?" Douglas Oliver said.

"Please."

Douglas Oliver poured, then frowned into his glass. "Where was I? Oh, yes…thirty years ago, we built a space port and opened this continent up to trade with the Empire. The Governor at the time didn't like it but there was nothing he could do to prevent it, not unless he wanted to embargo the Western Continent, and that really would have gone against their supposed principles. Many of the ships that trade with us also trade with the Eastern continent, and of course, we trade with the Eastern continent as well. We do manage to gather information.

"There are three separate Naval bases on the Eastern continent, each with its own Commander, all under the administration of Admiral Reynolds. Each base is at least semi-autonomous. The commander of the most Northern base is named Marcus Gerard. He's been there for nearly ten years. A year after his arrival, three young people in the nation of Kush disappeared." Douglas Oliver shrugged. "Kush is a desert, a harsh and difficult environment. People sometimes vanish. The sands swallow them and they are never seen again. I wouldn't have even known about it except that the Congress was in session at the time and one of the young people was the niece of the Representative from Kush.

"A year or so later, three more, again, all young, this time from the nation of Octavia. Octavia is mountainous. Treacherous terrain, mountains. There can be avalanches and rockslides and flash floods. I heard about this one because my wife is from Octavia. One of the people who vanished was the son of a co-worker of her aunt. There may have been more, perhaps many more, that I have never heard of but I now make it my business to pay attention to such things. Since then, there have been an additional thirty-seven young people, thirty-seven that I *know* of, teenagers, who vanished and whose bodies were never recovered, all from rural areas, never more than a very few from any one location. Never enough to arouse more than local suspicion." Douglas Oliver shrugged again. "Except for me, of course. I am definitely suspicious. Maybe it means nothing. Maybe it's all perfectly innocent—tragic, but innocent. In no case has there been evidence of anything amiss. There was no evidence at all. Still, I have trouble believing in this coincidence. The pattern has repeated itself too often." Douglas Oliver sipped his port and peered into the glass. "Captain Gerard rarely leaves his base. His ships patrol inward toward the spiral arm. There isn't much there, not according to the Second Empire, at least."

"There used to be," Michael said. "There are a lot of worlds in that direction that the First Empire settled."

"I know," Douglas Oliver said. He sipped his port. "Captain Gerard worries me."

The door opened. The waiter wheeled in a cart with two small soufflés in ramekins. "Eat it quickly," Douglas Oliver said, "before it collapses."

The soufflé was excellent. It dissolved in Michael's mouth, fruity, eggy, creamy and sweet.

"Your ship, if I am not mistaken, has shielding technology that the current Empire's vessels lack," Douglas Oliver said.

Michael nodded. "This is true."

Douglas Oliver smiled. Michael smiled back.

"Definitely something strange about that base," Romulus said. It was patrolled, for one thing, and this in an area almost devoid of other people. It was of course Empire policy to patrol, even in isolated areas, but this seemed...excessive. There was a high, electrified fence around the entire encampment. Armed guards and giant, mutated dogs made frequent walks around the perimeter. Unlike most guards in most places, these weren't just going through the motions. They paid attention.

The *London* hovered nearly thirty kilometers above the base, hidden from spy-eyes and sensors by its shields.

The tarmac contained twenty ships, eighteen of them corvettes nearly as large as the *London* and two destroyers, both considerably larger. One of the corvettes was obviously preparing to take off. Fuel had been loaded. Pallets of missiles and chaff and cartons of supplies had been carried on board. Finally, the crew marched from the barracks and up the ramp into the ship.

"A lot of crew for a ship that size," Romulus said.

Curly and Richard exchanged glances. Richard shrugged. Neither of them had any experience with naval ships and neither knew what size crew might be considered normal. Finally, the ship rose on its AG and headed out toward space.

The *London* could not be seen by the Second Empire sensors. They followed closely behind as the navy ship reached the transport point at the edges of the Illyrian system, and then vanished. Ships could not be followed in slipspace but their vector could be calculated by observation. After a few moments, Romulus said, "Apparently, they're going nowhere. There's nothing in that direction but inter-galactic space."

Which meant nothing, of course. If they wanted to confuse a pursuer, all they had to do was emerge at some random point, re-calculate a vector and be on their way to a new destination. Also, of course, there could be unregistered habitats deliberately placed in the middle of otherwise empty space, or they could be meeting up with another ship.

A few hours later, the *London* settled into its assigned berth and they took the ferry to Aphelion and their hotel. That evening, all of them had been invited to dinner at Douglas Oliver's mansion on the mainland. Michael was looking forward to it. Another ferry carried them across a calm sea. An armored limousine waited for them at the dock. A very large young man, carrying a gun at his hip and another under his arm, introduced himself as "Dustin," their driver, and they trooped into the car.

Two other cars, similarly armored and carrying four men each, drove along.

"A lot of security," Michael said.

Dustin smiled. "You can't be too careful. Guild Master Oliver is an important man."

"Are these precautions really necessary?"

A thoughtful look crossed Dustin's face. "It's been a couple of years since the last assassination attempt." Dustin shrugged. "It tends to discourage the ones who aren't serious."

Curly and Richard looked at each other. Gloriosa and Rosanna frowned. Catherine smiled.

"And the ones who are serious?" Michael asked.

"So far, none of them have survived."

Michael settled back into his seat. "Good to know."

The mansion was located in what appeared to be an enclave for the very wealthy. They were checked in through a gate in a high stone wall, then travelled down a paved road for about two kilometers. They passed three driveways, each surrounded by high fences and leading to large houses. Finally, they came to the end of the road, entered through a small security gate and pulled up in front of a very large house surrounded by a spacious lawn that ended in what appeared to be a cultivated forest. A circular brick stairway led up to the house. Douglas Oliver and a very tall, very beautiful woman, with honey blonde hair and an athletic figure waited for them at the top of the stairs.

"My wife, Jennifer," Douglas Oliver said.

They had all reviewed the data. Jennifer Mallet and Douglas Oliver had been married for nearly fifty years. They had seven children, the last two very young, the oldest three long since grown. Jennifer Oliver owned a successful corporation that manufactured athletic apparel and equipment.

Dinner was pleasant. The only other guests were Edward Lane, Oliver Industries' Executive Vice-President and Matthew and Marissa Oliver, Douglas and Jennifer's middle children, both in their early twenties and unmarried. Like most of the citizens of Meridien, they were large, athletic and ridiculously good looking.

Both Douglas and Jennifer seemed well versed in the minutiae of Empire politics, considerably more so than either Michael or his crew. "We've often thought of going off-world," Douglas said. He smiled at his wife. "But somehow, we've never seemed to have the time."

Jennifer shook her head. "We could have made the time but frankly, too much has always been going on."

Douglas Oliver smiled. "Jennifer is saying, as diplomatically as possible, that I'm indispensable."

Jennifer briefly raised her eyes to the ceiling and cleared her throat. Douglas Oliver's smile grew wider.

A few minutes later, Michael received a transmission from Romulus. "Six men in camouflage are trying to break into the ship."

Michael cleared his throat. "Excuse me," he said. "Might I use the facilities?"

"Down the corridor to the left," Jennifer said.

The bathroom was ornate, with two sinks and a sunken tub, but otherwise a standard design. Hopefully, his hosts were not so tawdry as to place bugs in the toilets. Once the door was locked, Michael said, "What's happening?"

"I notified the port authorities. A car containing eight security guards arrived within three minutes. The assailants have fled."

"Any damage?"

"None."

The landing field, a terminal and a security shack were the only things on the small island. There was no fence. "How did they arrive."

"A small boat."

"Where did the boat go?"

"It is heading in the direction of Aphelion. I have a drone following."

"Excellent," Michael said. "Perhaps I can arrange a reception."

"Wait," Romulus said. There was silence for nearly thirty seconds. "The boat has made rendezvous with a larger amphibious craft." Silence again for nearly a minute. "The boat has entered a large port in the craft's side. The craft has now arisen to three hundred meters and is flying out to sea, unfortunately, faster than my drone can follow."

"Out to sea," Michael muttered.

Romulus said nothing.

"Thank you," Michael said, and returned to the dining room.

The rest of the evening passed without incident. Near the end, Douglas Oliver said, "I imagine that your ship's functions are largely automated. Is that true?"

"It is."

"So then, you don't need a crew to operate the vessel, but you may need a crew to...how shall I say it...?" He smiled thinly. "Project force."

Michael glanced at Richard, Curly and the others. "That is correct," he said.

"How many would you like?"

"Are you offering?"

"Yes."

"Why?"

"Because I believe that we are on the same side. You are a soldier. " Douglas glanced at Michael's crew. "The rest of you, perhaps not so much. On this world, most of us spend some time as soldiers. We should support the soldiers who can be counted on."

Matthew and Marissa were following this exchange closely, as was Catherine Halliday. Jennifer glanced at her children and frowned.

Illyrian soldiers had been the best soldiers in the Empire. Michael imagined that if given the chance, they would be again. "Thank you," he said. "It's a generous offer. I'll certainly consider it."

Chapter 28

Over the next few days, three more ships took off from the Northern base, all heading for what seemed to be empty regions of space. Finally, on the eighth day, a corvette took off in the direction of a known destination.

"Tartarus-4," Romulus said. "A desert world. It was settled shortly before the Empire dissolved. According to the current data, it is low-tech and sparsely populated."

"Anything of value?"

"Dates, amber derived from the sap of a native tree. They're not a member of the Second Empire but they do trade."

Michael grunted. "Let's see."

Two days later, they emerged from slipspace and followed the Navy corvette toward the planet. The place was indeed low tech. The main city (barely a small town) was named Lidia. It contained perhaps eight-thousand people, mostly clustered in small huts along a sluggish river that led to a shallow sea. A dusty space-port contained two small ships, presumably merchant vessels. The place did have electricity, at least in the center of town, and running water, though Michael wouldn't want to try drinking it.

They hovered, invisible behind their shields, and watched as the corvette landed on the tarmac and were met by ten men in native dress and five from each of the two ships. A platoon of marines marched down the corvette's ramp, spread out and set up a perimeter along the field. A few minutes later, the corvette's captain, along with his lieutenant, came down the ramp. They stood to the side as fifty crew-members shepherded twenty-five AG sleds down the ramp, each containing one large crate. The crews of the merchant ships took five crates each. The natives took fifteen. The corvette's captain received what were apparently credit chips from the merchants and ten small wooden crates, presumably containing samples of Tartarus amber, from the natives.

A few minutes later, the corvette and the merchant ships rose into the air and vanished. The natives loaded their fifteen crates onto three battered trucks and drove down a dusty asphalt road toward the center of town.

The trucks were slow. The drones released from the *London*'s hold had no difficulty in keeping up. They drove to what appeared to be a warehouse by the river. The crates were unloaded and brought inside. The *London*'s drones released micro-drones, no larger than insects, which buzzed their way through the open doors. Inside, the crates were opened.

Rosanna drew a sharp breath. Gloriosa's face grew white, Richard's grim. Curly sighed. Each crate contained a body, apparently alive but asleep, with a small infusion pump attached to its right arm. The bodies were all young, all large, all in good shape.

"Slavers," Romulus said.

"Yes," Michael said, "and we've just stood by and watched while ten citizens of Illyria were flown away to God knows where."

"We didn't know," Rosanna said.

"We know, now."

Gloriosa looked at him, her eyes burning. "Are you going to stand for this?"

"No," Michael said. "I'm not."

Men with primitive weapons, knives and a few pistols that throw small lead bullets are not much competition for mechanized armor. They floated down from the ship and stepped through the open doorway of the warehouse, looking like monsters out of mythology.

The natives saw them and froze. "If you resist," Michael said, "we'll kill you." Generally, and in most circumstances, Michael preferred not to kill people. This time, he almost hoped that they did something stupid.

A few did. Most of them shook their heads, decided that they didn't like the odds and took a step back. Five tried to resist. Gloriosa put her fist through the chest of the largest. The chest made a sickening crunch. Blood bubbled up out of his mouth and he fell, dead at her feet. Rosanna, a bit more restrained, knocked out three with short, accurate punches. Curly picked up the fifth and slammed him to the ground. He didn't move again. The rest of the natives stared at them in silence until Michael said, "Put them back in the trucks. Gently." The natives looked at each other, shrugged and did as they were told.

As soon as the trucks reached the edge of town, the *London* shimmered into view above their heads, settled gently to the ground and lowered a ramp. Assisted by their armor, they had no difficulty carrying the fifteen sleeping bodies into the ship. They rose into the sky and set a course back to Illyria.

Chapter 29

They sat on a covered patio with a slate floor. The walls were entirely made out of glass and looked out on a swimming pool, and beyond the pool, a cultivated forest. Autumn was coming. The leaves had mostly turned yellow and orange and a scattering of brown, dried leaves lay across the plastic cover of the pool. Marisa and Matthew Oliver sat together on a couch, opposite their parents. Michael, the crew and Catherine Halliday sat facing them on wicker chairs.

Douglas Oliver was angry. The fifteen young people had awakened within a few hours of being brought into the *London*. Their stories were all identical. They had been alone or with small groups of friends. A flyer had hovered over them. They had been shot with some sort of dart and fallen unconscious.

"How many more that we don't know about?" Douglas Oliver said. "God *damn* it."

Jennifer looked worried. "How far does this extend? We can't fight the Empire."

"I think," Michael said, "that the Empire is going to have to fight itself."

"But will they?" Douglas asked.

Matthew shifted in his seat. So far, Matthew and his sister had listened attentively, kept their faces blank and said nothing—like soldiers.

Douglas looked at his son. "Yes?"

"Nothing," Matthew said.

Douglas smiled thinly. "Say what's on your mind."

"Mother is right. If the Governor and the Admiral are a part of this, we can't fight them, but we know that the Empire, the larger Empire is vehemently against slavery. Reliance will not tolerate this."

"So, you think we should let Reliance handle it?"

"Only as a last recourse," Marissa said. "We would lose considerable face if we do not at least attempt to handle our own problems."

Douglas gave his children an approving smile. "My three oldest children have been on Reliance for over a year. They're part of the team negotiating with the Empire." He turned to Michael. "As you said to me a few days ago, there are always factions but like you, we have found the Empire to be relatively reliable. The worlds under their sway are doing well. Their populations are not oppressed, or not very often, and not significantly so. The Empire abides by its own rules." He shrugged. "Mostly.

"We will prepare a report for Reliance. We will send that report on its way, and then we will approach both the Governor and the Admiral. And then we shall see."

Over the next three days, three merchant ships left Illyria, all carrying the same message for a number of different people. Their captains had dealt profitably with Douglas Oliver for years. He trusted them to safeguard their own interests. One way or another, he felt confident that the messages would be delivered.

"So," the Governor said. "You wanted to see me." He smiled at Michael and Douglas Oliver, inclined his head respectfully to Catherine Halliday.

Michael handed him a data-chip. "Is your equipment secure?"

The Governor shot him a keen glance. "Yes," he said.

"Look at this," Michael said. "Then we'll talk."

The Governor shrugged, plugged the chip in and scanned the screen. As he did so, his face turned slowly white. He glanced up at Douglas Oliver then his eyes returned to the screen. Finally, he sat back in his seat and drew a long sighing breath. "Marcus Gerard..."

Douglas and Michael looked at each other. "Marcus Gerard, most definitely, but can you be certain that Admiral Reynolds is not involved in this?" Michael said.

"Certain?" The Governor shook himself. "At this point, I don't think anything is certain, but I've known the Admiral for a long time. I do not believe that he would have anything to do with kidnapping and slave running. What would he have to gain?"

"What does Marcus Gerard have to gain?"

"A point," the Governor said. "Money, obviously, but you can't spend money if you're dead and the risks of exposure are enormous. He has to know that if these activities are discovered, he won't just be cashiered. He'll be executed. I can't imagine what it would take to keep an operation of this scope secret. How long has this been going on? How many of his people are involved?"

Michael had been wondering the same thing. "All of them, I suspect."

The Governor sat back in his chair. "What do we do now?" he muttered.

Douglas Oliver gave him a thin smile. "Set up a meeting with the Admiral. Don't tell him what it's about."

The capital city of the Eastern Continent was named Southron. Occupied primarily by civilian employees of the gigantic Southern Base, the city sprawled around the calm waters of Vermillion Bay and extended upward into the hills surrounding the harbor. The Base itself occupied a high plateau at the top of an extinct volcano.

The *London* sat on the landing field of Southron's civilian spaceport. The port was considerably larger than the city's small population would seem to require. Evidently, the Governor and his team were anticipating future growth.

For now, however, the *London* was almost alone. Only three other small ships, presumably merchants, occupied the enormous field.

"If the Governor betrays us, we could be dead tomorrow," Michael said.

Douglas Oliver sipped his coffee and shrugged. "The Governor was telling the truth. He knows nothing of this conspiracy."

Michael grinned. Damien Oliveros had always known when people were lying to him. So did Michael, though in his case, the enhancements that allowed this ability were artificial. So, apparently, did Douglas Oliver.

"Word, however, is going to leak out," Douglas Oliver said. "Then it will get interesting."

Interesting...that was one way of putting it.

Douglas Oliver looked at him. "You do realize that we may have to kill Admiral Reynolds, tomorrow?"

Michael, like Douglas Oliver, had been playing the game for a long time. "Of course," he said. If it came to that, if the Admiral were a part of this conspiracy, then it was likely that the Empire's entire military structure on Illyria was also irrevocably tainted. In that case, Michael, his crew, Catherine Halliday, plus Douglas Oliver and his family were going to have to vanish as quickly as possible into deep space. If they could. He sighed. "Let's hope it doesn't come to that."

The two of them, along with Catherine Halliday, were sitting in the *London*'s lounge, drinking coffee after one of Rosanna's excellent meals. The crew were playing poker at a large, circular table, along with Jennifer, Mathew and Marissa Oliver. Oliver's family gave the game their total attention. Their expressions were completely blank, their voices level. They didn't sigh. They didn't smile. They didn't blink. Rosanna had a tendency to frown when she had a bad hand. Curly would unconsciously swallow whenever he held more than a pair. Gloriosa was an open book. Only Richard had no tells, none that a normal person could see, at any rate, but even Richard could not control his heart beat. The Olivers apparently could.

Michael never played poker with his crew. It wouldn't be fair. The Olivers, however, seemed to have no such qualms.

Douglas Oliver looked over at the table and grinned. "Like candy from a baby," he said.

Michael shrugged. "They'll learn."

"Admiral," Douglas Oliver said.

The Admiral frowned. "Mr. Oliver, Captain Glover, what can I do for you?" He glanced at the Governor.

The Admiral seemed honestly curious and not at all anxious. That was reassuring.

The Governor handed the Admiral a folder. "Read this," he said. "We'll wait."

The Admiral looked at the folder, shrugged, sat down and opened it. His eyes widened. He glanced up at Douglas Oliver, then returned his attention to the folder. He went through every page, saying nothing, glancing back occasionally at a previous document. When he had finished, he closed the folder and sighed. His face was gray. "How did you get this?" he asked.

"The *London*'s shielding is impervious to your sensors. We followed them."

"You? You, personally?"

"Yes, of course," Michael said. "And my crew."

The Admiral made a sour face. "I guess there's no chance of a mistake, then. Too bad…"

"No," Michael said. "I assure you that there is no mistake. Would you like to question the people that we've rescued?" They were being held in protective custody in Meridien. Their parents had been informed that their children were safe but were given no circumstances of their capture or rescue.

"That won't be necessary." The Admiral slumped in his seat, then shook his head. "God damn this son-of-a-bitch…"

The Governor nodded. Douglas Oliver and Michael said nothing. Finally, the Admiral sighed and rose to his feet. "Let's move," he said.

"Right now?" Michael asked.

The Admiral nodded. "Absolutely. As fast as we possibly can. Before somebody leaks. Before they can organize a defense."

Michael glanced at Douglas, who nodded. Nice that they didn't have to murder the Admiral. That would have caused complications…

Michael sat in the central chair on the *London*'s Command Deck, an induction helmet feeding him a real-time spherical view of space surrounding the ship. Appearing straight ahead in the view that the helmet fed into his awareness, though in reality kilometers beneath them, sat the Northern Base.

Three tiers of padded seats circled the room. His crew, plus Douglas Oliver, Jennifer, Matthew and Marissa, sat in the seats, observing. Three dimensional holographs, a larger but slightly less detailed version of what the helmet showed Michael, floated above their heads.

The Admiral knew his business. On his command, swiftly and without question, the Southern fleet had mobilized and taken to the skies, twenty-seven corvettes, four destroyers, two frigates and one enormous battleship, nearly three hundred meters in length. They flew in a cone formation, with the *Firedrake*, the battleship that also served as the Admiral's flagship at the cone's tip. The fleet had circumnavigated the entire world, coming at Marcus Gerard's base from the North. It added a few minutes to the flight but hopefully would serve to arouse less suspicion.

Regardless, it was apparent that their arrival was not quite a surprise.

Admiral Reynolds' voice came clearly to Michael's ears. "The Northern Fleet is mobilizing. As we surmised, they've had advance warning." After this was over, assuming that they won, identifying all the spies, traitors and informers in their midst was going to be a bitch. Thankfully, that wasn't Michael's problem.

The Admiral did not seem disturbed by the enemy mobilization. He seemed relieved. They had been afraid that the base would already be deserted, Marcus Gerard, his ships and his men vanished without a clue. Instead, Michael could clearly see the last remaining troops marching from the Northern base and entering the ships. As he watched, they floated upward, toward the Southern Fleet.

"Captain Gerard." The Admiral's voice came clearly through the ship's intercom. Clearly, the Admiral wanted every man and woman in both fleets to hear him. "You are relieved of your command. I order all ships of the Northern Fleet to cease your mobilization and return to your base."

Not a single ship responded. Beneath them, the fleet formed a cone and stormed upward. As they came, the cone rotated and as each ship faced toward the Southern Fleet, it released a hail of missiles.

Lasers flicked out, aimed at the oncoming missiles, which disappeared in balls of expanding flame. Perhaps a third of the missiles made it through the laser fire, impacting on the Southern Fleet's shields. The shields flickered but held.

Marcus Gerard had fewer ships than the Southern Fleet, with only one destroyer and one frigate. He had no chance of winning. Apparently, he had decided to go down fighting.

"Fire at will," the Admiral said. A storm of missiles sped toward the approaching ships, which seemed determined to plow through them. The missiles impacted on the Fleet's combined screens and flared bright red.

"There," Michael said. Far below them, almost two kilometers outside the perimeter of the base, an enormous metal plate slid to the side and a large hole appeared in the ground. Three ships rose together, a frigate and two destroyers, their shields interlinked. They flew upward at an oblique angle, away from the battle, heading for deep space.

If the ships of the Southern Fleet noticed, there was nothing they could do. The Southern Fleet had its own problems. The Northern Fleet came steadily onward. As they neared, the Southern cone widened and re-formed into a cylinder. The Northern Fleet, lasers and missiles firing, flew straight into the mouth of the cylinder, which returned fire at point blank range. One by one, the Northern Fleets' shields failed and went down, each ship vanishing in an expanding hail of fragments.

Within an hour, not a single ship remained of Marcus Gerard's fleet.

The Admiral's face flickered into Michael's awareness. "Well?" the Admiral asked. "What did you think of that?"

"Easier than it should have been," Michael said.

The Admiral grinned ferociously. "I suspect that they were putting on a show. Those ships were piloted by drones. I agree with you. It was all too easy. I think that their people have escaped."

"Three ships stayed back. Big ones. They left during the battle."

The Admiral nodded. "It's what we expected. Were you able to track them?"

"Yes," Michael said. "They're heading for the Rift."

Chapter 30

They stayed well away from the Northern Base and let the drones go in first. None of them would have been surprised if the place had been set to self-destruct. This proved not to be the case, however. The Admiral was hopeful that at least some useful information would be discovered. Michael less so. In the end, Michael proved correct. The Northern Base had been scrubbed clean, the command center firebombed, all of the computers and databases thoroughly destroyed. The barracks yielded a few personal effects of a few low-level personnel. Supposedly, the records were kept in duplicate at the Southern Base but none of these could be trusted, not any longer. Were Marcus Gerard and any of his people who they were supposed to be? And if not, who were they?

They did manage to isolate some fragments of DNA, none of which matched any of their records, but that proved very little. Legitimate military personnel could have had legitimate guests. Curious, though, that not one single soldier supposedly assigned to the Northern Base left even the smallest identifiable fragment.

Between the Southern and Northern Bases lay Fort Talmadge, named for the long since retired Admiral who had first re-established contact with Illyria. Fort Talmadge was commanded by Nial Ferguson, an officer whose career to this point had been exemplary. Admiral Reynolds had made a strategic decision to keep Nial Ferguson and his people out of the loop.

Now, the Southern Fleet hovered over Fort Talmadge. Nial Ferguson's bewildered face peered out of the holograph, relayed to them from the *Firedrake*.

"Captain," the Admiral said. "I am ordering you and all of your people to leave your weapons behind and exit Fort Talmadge. Take nothing with you except the clothes that you're wearing. Do it now."

Captain Ferguson cleared his throat. "Yes, sir," he said.

The holograph vanished. Three minutes later, the base began to empty and the Admiral's people swooped in. The bewildered soldiers of Fort Talmadge were searched. None were found to be carrying weapons. Pre-fab housing was established. An electrified fence was set up. One by one, Nial Ferguson's people were questioned, their identities confirmed, their DNA and fingerprints checked against the database.

All of them were exactly who they were supposed to be. All who were present, at any rate. Five, it turned out, were missing.

"Two lieutenants, two lieutenant-commanders and a commander," the Admiral said. He grimaced. "And from the Southern Base, a lieutenant, three lieutenant-commanders and two commanders are also missing."

"Smart," Michael said. "High enough in the chain of command to have free rein. They could go anywhere and nobody was going to question them."

"Not enough of them to take over," Douglas Oliver said, "but enough to gather information."

Governor Truscott sipped his tea, swirled the liquid in the cup and frowned down at it. "Enough to commit quite a bit of sabotage, too, if it came to that."

Now that the battle was done, the Admiral seemed deflated. Michael couldn't blame him. A scapegoat was going to be necessary. The Admiral may or may not have been able to prevent the enemy infiltration of their forces but he was going to get the blame. Somebody had to and it might as well be the man in charge. The Admiral sighed. Luckily, he had already reached retirement age.

"So, who were they?" Douglas Oliver said.

"We know who they were supposed to be. Who were they, really? Not a clue," the Admiral said. "All of them come from very distant worlds. Their families will be questioned, of course, but I suspect that these supposed families, if they exist at all, will have never heard of them." He shook his head and lapsed into silence.

"Are we otherwise agreed, then?" Michael said.

The Admiral sighed. Then after a moment, he said, "About Catherine Halliday and her little problem? Certainly. Why not?"

"Yes," the Governor said. "The people of Chronos will be welcomed. The knowledge that they carry is extraordinarily valuable. As for the rest of it…" He frowned at the Admiral, who sat morosely at the table and ignored him, "that will be up to High Command."

Douglas Oliver smiled. "And what are you going to do, now?" he said to Michael.

Michael smiled back. "I've always wanted to see the Rift."

"Fine with me," Curly said. Rosanna shrugged. Richard and Gloriosa exchanged a glance that Michael could not interpret. Both of them nodded.

Michael wondered when it was, exactly, that he had begun to depend upon his crews' opinion. It certainly had not worked that way during his former life. The Captain of the ship was the leader of the enterprise. He determined their destination and their goal, he alone. Still, Michael was no longer in the military, he reminded himself, despite his "retainership" with the Empire. It seemed only fair to give them a voice. They didn't have to stay with him. They were free agents. They could leave at any time. None of them seemed inclined to do so, however, and he had found, somewhat to his own surprise, that he enjoyed having them around, as weirdly mismatched as they all seemed to be.

Catherine Halliday had already left the ship. She was the ambassador of her people, after all, and those people would, if things went well, be arriving within a very few months. Her place was here. She had purchased a small house near the center of Southron and already moved her few possessions into it. She had smiled at Michael, then stepped close and kissed his cheek.

"Be well," she said, "and thank you."

Michael nodded. He found that he had difficulty speaking. He watched her as she walked away. She didn't look back.

They were scheduled to leave in the morning but that night, they dined once again at the Oliver estate. The meal was again excellent. Douglas and his wife, Michael noted, had almost a private language of their own. They smiled frequently at each other, seeming to convey a wealth of meaning with no more than a glance.

They had been married for a very long time. Michael sipped his really excellent wine and pondered the two of them. It must be nice, he thought. Then he smiled to himself. On the other hand, you could get very, very tired of another person after fifty years. That did not seem to be the case with Jennifer and Douglas Oliver, however. Not at all.

"So," Douglas said, once the last course had been served, "You're heading toward the Rift. Have you given any thought to my proposal?"

"More men?" Michael glanced at his crew. Curly raised his glass and nodded. Rosanna smiled. Gloriosa frowned and Richard remained impassive. "I have. Considering where we've already been and where we plan on going in the immediate future, it seems like a good idea. What exactly are you offering?"

Matthew and Marissa raised their heads, suddenly attentive. Douglas smiled at them. "I've been talking to my people. A fair number of them would welcome the chance to go off-world. They're all well-trained. How many would you like?"

How many would it take to take over the ship? Did he trust Douglas Oliver? He remembered Damien Oliveros very well. Brilliant, ruthless when he had to be, but a man who kept his word. Douglas Oliver was not Damien Oliveros, of course, despite having his memories. Michael admired Douglas Oliver. He even liked him, but he had no reason to trust him. Still, the *London* had resources that no citizen of Illyria, or even a citizen of the Second Empire could know of.

He pondered the question, noted Matthew and Marissa's eager faces. "How about twenty?"

"How about twenty-two?" Douglas said.

Matthew grinned. Marissa drew a small, barely audible breath.

Michael looked at them. "And are you also well-trained?" Michael said.

"Very," Matthew said. Marissa nodded.

"Are you looking for excitement? It might not be as exciting as you seem to think. I hope not, actually."

"It will be different," Marissa said. She had a low, husky voice. It occurred to Michael that until this moment, he had rarely heard her speak. She grinned. "And maybe it will be as exciting as we think."

The *London*'s new crew settled in below decks, where the accommodations held space for nearly two-hundred. The twenty men and women that Douglas Oliver had given him had plenty of room. They came with their own internal organization and Michael felt it best not to change that. Their sergeant was Dustin Nye, the man who had driven Michael and his crew on their visits to the

145

Oliver estate. All of them were big and fit. They moved slowly but with deliberate precision. Their eyes missed very little. They resembled in all ways the men and women with whom Michael had served for so many years, so many years ago.

All of this made the official organization of the ship's contingent somewhat awkward. Michael had taken to referring to Curly and the rest as his "crew," though in fact, none had assigned duties other than Rosanna, the cook, and no chain of command had been established other than the simple acknowledgement that Michael was in charge. Now, with more people as part of the equation, the arrangement, formerly comfortable, seemed inadequate.

The status of Matthew and Marissa Oliver also presented a problem. Both had served time in the Meridien Guard, as did all citizens of that nation. At various times, they had taken instruction from Dustin and, Michael was given to understand, had served under Dustin's command during two violent episodes in the recent past when competing business interests had attempted to encroach upon Oliver Enterprises. At all other times, however, both were the children of the boss, and used to being treated as such.

"Sit down," Michael said.

Matthew and Marissa glanced at each other. Michael was sitting at his desk. He wanted to deliver the message that this was not a casual discussion. Matthew and Marissa both sat.

"First of all," Michael said. "Would it be better for you to stay with your father's people?"

Matthew frowned, thinking it over. "We don't when we're at home," Marissa said.

"If you're worried that the men might be resentful, then don't be," Matthew said. "They understand that rank has its privileges."

Well, that was the issue, wasn't it? "I'm sure that they do," Michael said. "The question is, who outranks who?"

"Whom," Marissa said, and blushed. "Sorry," she said.

Michael gave her a long look. She dropped her eyes.

"I've had a very small crew up to this point," Michael said. "The ship is fully automated. I don't really need a crew other than, as your father put it, to 'project force.' I haven't had a chain of command because I didn't need one. I don't know if I need one now. So, here's what we're going to do. You will be given rooms on the main deck, like Curly, Rosanna and the others. Dustin is in charge of his people. I am in charge of Dustin and everybody else. You are allowed to question my decisions in private, never in public. When I give an order, it is to be obeyed. Is that clear?"

"Certainly," Matthew said.

"Of course." Marissa nodded. "Mom and Dad run a tight ship. We understand that you're in charge."

"Very well," Michael said. "We'll see how it works out. If I have to make changes, I will."

The Rift was a volume of warped space between two spiral arms. Strange things were seen there. Strange things happened there.

Two advanced alien species inhabited small Confederations of their own, just across the rift, in the opposite spiral arm. Transit across the rift was considered hazardous but the trade was lucrative. Most ships emerged unscathed but some had reported unexpected, random pulses of energy and unexplained turbulence in space. One ship had landed with what appeared to be claw marks in her titanium hull. Two had landed with crews almost catatonic with fear, though none could ever remember what it was that had frightened them. A few ships had simply vanished. The center of the rift contained a spinning torus of energy, two rotating neutron stars obscured by a haze of cosmic dust, visible from many light years away and covering most of the horizon from the few planets perched on its edge that humans could inhabit. There were many questions regarding the Rift whose answers were unknown but the navy felt it prudent to assume that what could not be understood might possibly represent a threat. One of the largest naval bases in the Empire was located on Helios, a dwarf planet circling a red dwarf star less than one light month from the rift's edge.

The economy of Helios depended upon two factors: the navy and tourism. Intelligent beings came from all the known worlds to look upon the twisting, glowing lights of the rift, a perpetual, silent fireworks display. Why should Michael and his crew be any different?

Helios orbited in the habitable zone of its tiny star but was, in its natural state, too small to maintain an atmosphere. A speck of neutronium at the little world's center fixed that and Helios had since been extensively terra-formed.

Their approach to the planet was routine. If the enemy, whoever this nameless enemy happened to be, had infiltrated the local authorities, it was not apparent. They settled into their appointed berth at the civilian spaceport.

"You can assign leave however you like," Michael told Dustin. "Make sure at least five remain on the ship."

"Will do," Dustin said. "The men will appreciate it."

The port was located nearly ten kilometers from the center of the city. The port had its own terminal and a train came by every hour or so, but Michael decided to find more central accommodations. He checked into a hotel high on a ridge overlooking a medium sized lake, accompanied by Curly, Rosanna, Richard, Matthew and Marissa. Gloriosa preferred, this time, to stay with the ship.

Michael used to enjoy fishing when he was young and the lake was supposedly stocked with mutated giant bass. He hoped that he would find some time to try his luck.

They arrived in the late afternoon and met a few hours later in the dining room, which had a high ceiling and enormous picture windows, all of which afforded a generous view of the sky. As the sun vanished beneath the horizon, the lights in the sky grew brighter, constant but ever changing, first purples and reds, then blue mixed with yellow and green. Roiling, silent clouds swept across the horizon, drenched in color.

All of them stared upward, smiling in delight.

The meal was excellent. They soon finished and after a few more minutes looking into the Rift, they went to bed.

"Right this way, sir."

The base looked comfortably familiar, the buildings made out of red brick, three stories high, with neatly trimmed flowers and hedges along concrete foundations, all surrounded by iron fencing. The little receptionist wore a light brown Marine uniform, with Corporal's chevrons on the shoulders. Her smile was wide, her eyes curious as she led the way to an office at the end of the hallway. She knocked. A voice said, "Come," and she poked her head in the door.

"Mr. Glover, sir."

"Thank you, Corporal."

The man sitting behind the desk appeared middle-aged but trim, with closely cut brown hair and deep blue eyes. He wore the bars of a Navy Captain on his shoulders. His official title was Director of Intelligence.

"Mr. Glover, please sit down. I'm Captain James Weston. You wished to see me?"

Michael smiled. "Code Three-X-Seventeen-Dash-Fourteen-Z," he said.

The Captain looked startled. "Don't hear that one very much. Give me a second. His eyes slid to his holo screen. His eyebrows raised. "Alright," he said. "So, what can I do for you?"

"Please review this. Then we'll talk." He handed a data chip to the Captain, who raised an eyebrow, weighing the chip in his hand, then he slid it into a slot on his interface and concentrated on the screen as he absorbed the information.

"Captain Lanier made a good bargain." Weston sat back and stared at Michael's face. "Your solution to this rickety little Empire was most creative." He grinned. "Let's hope it works out as you expect. If it doesn't, firmer measures will have to be taken."

"I did what I could," Michael said, "and I warned them."

The Captain shrugged. "We'll see. As to the events on Illyria, that is much more worrisome. We have also had our incidents. Pirate activity has been steadily increasing in this sector. I don't like the fact that the renegades seemed to flee in this direction, but by now, they could be anywhere." He frowned. "We shall certainly be on our guard."

They chatted for a few more minutes. The Captain offered coffee. Michael thanked him but refused, and after a few minutes more, he excused himself and made his way back to the hotel.

A good day's work, he thought. He was pleased to note that since a few hours before, his credit balance had increased, as specified in his contract with the Navy. In addition, Captain Westin had added a finder's bonus for two new worlds. A good day's work, indeed.

Helios was attacked the next day. Three small ships, masquerading as trading vessels, opened fire on the sensor grid while three other ships dropped down onto an amusement park. Thirty men wearing light armor and carrying rifles marched out, set up a cordon around the periphery of the park and herded the terrified tourists into a large open space in the park's center. The on-site Security was quickly overwhelmed. One by one, the youngest, prettiest women and youngest, healthiest men were separated out and escorted by armed pirates into the ships. Over one hundred were taken. A few of the men tried to resist. They were casually shot, once in the chest, once more in the head, and their bodies left where they had fallen.

Two more ships lobbed missiles at the nearest Navy installation. The base's screens prevented the missiles from doing any damage but the attack delayed the military response long enough for all the ships to escape, heading into the center of the Rift.

The attack took place over two hundred kilometers from their hotel. Michael and the others were unaware of any trouble until it was long over, but the media talked of little else during the next few hours. The military tried to control the flow of information but the basic facts were beyond dispute.

The mood that evening was subdued. The lights of the Rift seemed suddenly ominous, concealing dangers both known and unknown. The diners tended to concentrate on their meals, not looking up at the endless sky. "The Navy will have to respond," Rosanna said.

"No doubt," Michael replied.

"What are we going to do?"

A slow smile spread over Michael's face. "We're civilians. What could we do?"

Richard snorted into his soup. Matthew frowned, first at Richard, then Michael. Curly stolidly chewed his food. Marissa looked eager. "Curly and I signed on to see the Universe," Rosanna said. "It's been interesting so far."

Curly swallowed a piece of his steak. "We've come to know you pretty well. You're not going to sit around doing nothing."

They were all looking at him. "Okay," Michael said. "The plan is very simple..."

Chapter 31

It took less than a day for the Navy to organize their response. A fleet of twelve light, fast corvettes, plus six destroyers and three frigates set out for the Rift. The *London* trailed behind them.

"They're going to send a fleet," Michael had said. "They'll have to. We have only one ship with no obvious military capability, and we're still considered civilians. They're not going to ask us to help and they wouldn't let us if we offered. We're going to trail along behind and see what happens."

Random pulses of energy battered at their sensors but it was nothing that the ship couldn't handle. Inside the Rift itself, the lights were much brighter than they appeared from Helios.

They sat in the ship's lounge, reading, playing games and occasionally staring through the monitor screens at the ferocious bursts of energy bathing this region of space. Richard Norlin played the piano, which they had moved from the cargo hold into the main lounge. The music reflected his mood, sometimes ominous and slow, sometimes loud and exuberant. He played Chopin or Tchaikovski or Brandt or Ishikawa but he always came back to rock and roll. Michael had never heard of Elvis Presley, Roy Orbison, Little Richard or Jerry Lee Lewis, but Richard loved them. Whatever he played, the music seemed to flow directly from Richard's own soul, his touch on the keyboard deft and sure.

Michael listened, wondering for a brief moment how anybody could have ever considered Richard Norlin to be stupid...but then, he didn't have to wonder. Richard had been arrogant, hostile, passive aggressive and a drunkard, all because he had been placed on a life course that he despised. He had no interest in politics. The prospect of becoming the Duke of Norlin disgusted him. Now, the pressure to conform to his society's expectations was off. Now, he could be himself, and more than anything else, Richard Norlin was a man who played music.

All of them listened, their other cares forgotten, at least for a few moments, and finally, when the last faint note had sputtered out and Richard rose to his feet and shyly smiled at them, none of them said a word. Through the screens, the lights of the Rift roiled and fluttered.

It was not possible to follow or even detect another ship in slipspace, but the Navy fleet had made no secret of their intentions. They were heading for the torus of energy that marked the very center of the Rift. The torus had been explored, centuries ago, and the data from those expeditions still existed. Two neutron stars slowly spiraling around each other, a haze of dust obscuring the center, probably the remnants of shattered worlds, and around it all, an Oort cloud of comets and asteroids that stretched for trillions of kilometers. It was assumed that the pirates had a base somewhere in the cloud.

"Emergence in three seconds," Romulus stated. "Three, two, one…"

Ahead of them, the lights of the Rift flickered. "Rocks," Romulus said. "As far as the instruments can detect, nothing but rocks. The energy background is constant."

Constant but enough to burn any unshielded vessel to a molten, blackened crisp. "The fleet?" Michael asked.

"They have emerged and are re-grouping, two light-minutes ahead of us."

"Good. We'll follow them."

Asteroid belts, though dense by the standards of the vacuum, are still mostly empty. They swerved now and then to avoid a particularly large rock but had no difficulty following the Empire fleet. An hour later, two of the ships vanished into slipspace, then two more.

All four ships re-appeared after a few hours. The fleet changed direction very slightly. The *London* continued to follow. "Records indicate a small, dwarf planet twelve hours ahead, over five hundred kilometers in diameter," Romulus said.

Sleets of radiation splattered against their shields as they moved toward the torus. The lights ahead grew steadily brighter. The ship's brain increased the filters on their screens and then increased them again.

The fleet separated into three groupings, each arranged around one of the frigates. Michael and the others stared at the monitors as the fleet approached the rocky little world. "Anything?" Michael asked.

"No," Romulus replied. "The planetoid appears to be dead." Romulus tilted his head to the side. "Wait," he said. "Now, I'm picking up something."

The three groups of ships grew closer together, oriented toward a spot on the surface. "They appear to have identified a target," Michael said.

"There," Romulus said. He pointed. "In the shadow."

The side of the world that faced outward from the torus was dark, except for a series of concentric, yellow lights midway between the world's pole and the equator. "Domes," Romulus said.

A green light appeared on the planetoid's surface, licking up at the first grouping of ships. "Apparently, they are hostile," Romulus said.

Romulus, Michael thought, sometimes tended to belabor the obvious. It was a fault common to non-organic minds. "You think?"

Curly grimaced. Rosanna flicked her eyes toward the robot, then back to the screen.

Emitting sudden, brief puffs of flame, at least three hundred missiles emerged from the surface and jetted toward the oncoming fleet. Balls of glowing plasma and lasers flicked outward from the ships, pinpointing the oncoming missiles, which exploded one-by-one in fiery bursts. The ships spiraled in toward the surface.

"How extensive is this base?" Michael said.

"Large," Romulus said. "There are four domes, each over five hundred meters in diameter. I cannot tell how far underground the installation might extend. Presumably, they connect beneath the surface."

"If they want to get the prisoners back, they're going to have to land and root them out. They can't just stand off and bomb the place."

Apparently, the expedition's leader had come to the same conclusion. The ships spread out and touched down beneath the horizon line in a circle around the four glowing domes. Small ports opened in each ship. Grapples shot downward, anchoring the ships into the planetoid's soil.

A sudden, enormous burst of light blinded their instruments. All of them stared at the screens. "What is happening?" Michael asked.

Romulus remained silent. After a few seconds, the lights faded away and they could see...nothing. There was nothing left to see. Where the small, round world had been, nothing remained but a cloud of expanding rocks. The little world, the enemy base and all the Empire ships were gone.

"A matter/anti-matter explosion," Romulus said. "Presumably, the base had already been abandoned. This was a trap."

"Really?" Michael muttered. He shook his head and drew a deep breath. "We'll spend a little time looking for survivors, then head back to Helios. The Navy will want to know what happened here."

Curly gave him an incredulous look.

"Nobody could have lived through that," Rosanna said. Matthew and Marissa stared at the screen, their faces white.

"No," Michael said. "No, I'm sure you're right, but I want to be able to say that we did everything we could."

Richard shook his head and shrugged.

"There are energy signatures on our screens," Romulus said. "At least twenty of them, approximately ten light-seconds away."

"Enemy ships?"

"No, too diffuse for that. The energy is scattered but nowhere near high enough for ships. I have no record of anything like this."

The shifting lights of the Rift and the bright, glowing ball of the torus shone on their screens. Nothing else. "Are they approaching?"

"No. Not yet. Their distance from the *London* is remaining constant."

Michael shrugged. "Let's be about our business and get out of here."

Three hours later, they had gone through all the rubble. No evidence remained of anything made by man. The base, the ships and whatever else had once existed on the little world had been vaporized. Nothing remained but rocks and dust, expanding outward into the Rift.

"Energy signatures are now coming closer," Romulus said. "I am detecting sensor pings. We are under observation." They stared at the monitor screens. Slowly, a huge, diaphanous ovoid could be made out, translucent, transmitting the lights of the Rift through enormous fan-like wings, spreading more than fifty kilometers across. Another appeared, then another.

They stared, enrapt. "What are those things," whispered Richard.

"Romulus?" Michael asked.

"Light sails."

"Focus on the center."

The image on the screen enlarged, then enlarged again. Between each two light sails, an amorphous, egg-shaped mass seemed to vibrate and churn. Multi-colored lights, reflecting the lights of the Rift, ran across each surface.

"Perhaps these are artifacts left by some alien race, or perhaps they themselves represent life of an unknown variety," Romulus said. "Where there is matter and energy, there is always the possibility of life. I cannot tell."

Life was persistent, Michael reflected. Living beings floated in the methane oceans of gas giants, like enormous, balloon-like whales. Sentient rock-like entities had been discovered on tiny worlds so far from their primary that their sun appeared no larger than a distant star. Matter plus energy could organize itself in ways that humanity could barely conceive.

"Are they intelligent?" Gloriosa asked.

"Perhaps," Romulus said. "Or perhaps not, and perhaps their intelligence is so far removed from ours that the concept is meaningless."

"You could just say you don't know," Gloriosa muttered.

The sails began to fold inward as they drew closer to the *London*. Soon, each metallic center was covered with a thin, translucent shroud. Twenty-two of them circled the ship in a hollow cylindrical formation. A cube about two meters on a side floated sedately down the center of the cylinder. The cube stopped ten meters from their outer screens. Slowly, one-by-one, each metallic, ovoid mass turned and drifted away from the *London*.

"Their sails are furled," Richard said. "How can they move."

"They appear to be utilizing the negative propulsion of vacuum energy, similar to the principal behind our own gravity generators."

They waited. Soon, the enormous alien beings were gone beyond the range of their sensors, leaving just the cube. They stared at it through the screens, solid, silent and unmoving. "And what is that?" Michael asked.

"I don't know," Romulus said. "Give me a moment."

"Whatever it is, I think it would be wiser to leave it," Richard said.

Michael frowned, uncertain.

"If they had wanted to attack us, they could have already done so," Gloriosa said.

Matthew appeared troubled. Marissa glanced at her brother, then back to the image in the screen. "Romulus?" Michael said.

"I am scanning it's interior." Romulus appeared to hesitate. "The young lady is correct. It would appear to pose no threat."

"What is it?"

"A refrigeration chamber." Romulus glanced at Michael. "It contains a body in stasis."

"Human?"

"Not exactly."

"What is its composition?"

"Carbon, hydrogen and oxygen, some trace minerals. It is organic. If awakened, it would appear to be able to survive in the environment of this ship."

Curly raised his brow and shrugged. Richard shook his head, looking doubtful. Michael slowly grinned. "Let's bring it aboard."

Chapter 32

It was smaller than most humans, not remarkably so, but the rest of it could never be mistaken for human. Its skin was a dull, uniform gray, without nipples, freckles or any other markings. Hairless, with tiny ears set close to its skull, its nose was a mere slit, the legs and arms long and attenuated. It did have a mouth in the appropriate place in the skull, and eyes, though the pupil covered almost the entire globe and the sclera, what could be seen of it, was bright orange. Where the genitals should have been, there was only a small, fleshy tube, perhaps one-centimeter in length, and no discernible gonads.

It lay on the bed, eyes closed, chest rising slowly.

"Internal organs," Romulus said, "are approximately human normal."

"Approximately?"

"The liver is larger than standard but this does not appear to be a pathological condition. I would estimate that such an organ would be quite efficient at clearing toxins from the system. Also, the brain, though average in size, appears to have an increased number of sulci and gyri, which would correlate to a significantly increased intelligence. The lungs are also enlarged, and the hemoglobin is almost entirely a variant which releases oxygen to the tissues more readily than normal, similar to Hemoglobin F. In sum, this body is designed to thrive in difficult environments."

Similar, Michael thought, to his own enhancements. "Brain activity?"

"The body is still cold. Probably soon," Romulus said.

It opened its eyes an hour later and an hour after that, made its first sounds. These were formless, almost toneless, not words as human beings understood them.

It had seemed wiser to isolate this strange being until its intentions were known. It lay in bed, a large monitor screen suspended on the wall, through which they could all watch it, and it could watch them.

"Do you have a name?" Gloriosa asked.

Its mouth closed. It grew silent and seemed to consider the question. "You are on the ship, *London*," she said. "The ship is named for an ancient city on the planet Earth. London no longer exists. Isn't that silly? Naming a ship for a city that no longer exists."

It cocked its head to the side. An intent expression appeared on its face. It made a brief, atonal sound.

"My name is Michael Glover," Michael said. "I'm the owner and captain of this ship." Actually, Michael was not entirely certain that this was true, but there seemed to be no one left with a better claim. "Curly?"

"My name is Curly Brice. Crew."

They introduced themselves in order. "My name is Rosanna Devereaux. I am also crew."

"My name is Richard Norlin."

It lay in bed, monitors attached to its chest and torso, frowned and appeared to clear its throat. "Name," it said.

Gloriosa clapped her hands together in delight and nodded her head up and down.

It nodded back.

Within two hours, it had an adequate grasp of Basic. They brought it an interface, which it accessed directly through implant jacks in its skull. The implant jacks were a surprise. For one thing, they had not been there an hour before; for another, humanity had given up such modifications millennia ago, following the self-destruction of the Vortigern Anocracy after their brains were hacked by a syndicate of rogue AI's. Nevertheless, for rapid assimilation of large amounts of data, implant jacks worked exceptionally well.

It smiled, though, and nodded, when Romulus presented him with the interface. "Thank you," it said. "This will be most helpful."

They left it alone for the rest of the afternoon, while the *London* surged through slipspace toward Helios. A few hours later, as they were sitting down to dinner, it emerged from its room. Since they had last seen it, it had grown nearly ten centimeters. Its skin was no longer gray. It had formed a nose and dark brown hair was beginning to sprout on its head. It looked male. They all stared at it as it approached the table.

"Please sit down," Michael said.

"Thank you," it said, and took a chair next to Richard Norlin. "This is delightful." It smiled.

"Potatoes?" Michael said.

Its smile grew wider. "Please. I'm eager to sample all of the food items described in your databanks. My people do not eat food as you do."

"What do they do?" Gloriosa asked.

"We ingest energy directly. There's a lot of it around."

"Oh," Gloriosa said. She sank back in her seat, frowning.

The meal passed in awkward silence. They concentrated on the food on their plates and tried to ignore the stranger in their midst. For its part, it sampled every dish with intense concentration.

"So," Michael said, when they had all eaten their fill. "What are you?"

It gave them a wide smile. "I am an avatar. My people live for many thousands of years. Other races rarely enter the vicinity of the torus but humanity has repeatedly done so. This body was cloned from human DNA and one of the people of the Rift split its consciousness, a part of which now resides within me."

"And why," Michael asked, "are you here?"

"I have been given a mission. I am to accompany you to the human worlds and gather information."

Ominous, Michael thought. He briefly considered killing the avatar and dropping its body into space but decided to keep that idea in reserve. "To what purpose?"

"My people are uncertain as to humanity's intentions. Some of you have been observed to act with unreasonable violence, which disturbs us. Consideration has been given to eliminating mankind, but this would probably be beyond our capabilities."

Good to know. Michael poured some sherry into a delicate crystal glass and sipped it, then asked. "What other options have you considered?"

The no longer small figure gave a shrug. "Embargo, disassociation, limited trade, full diplomatic relations." It frowned. "Is that the correct term: diplomatic relations?"

"It will do," Michael said.

"As of now, no options have been ruled out."

"You look different," Rosanna said, "than when you arrived."

It smiled. "My protoplasm has been designed to be adaptable. Now that I have read your literature and history, I am taking the form of a human male, the better to blend in."

"Not a female?" Gloriosa asked.

"Is that a mistake?" It frowned. "From what I have read, males would seem to have more latitude in many of your societies."

Rosanna gave a minute shrug. Curly cleared his throat. Matthew laughed silently and glanced at his sister. Gloriosa glowered and stared at Richard Norlin. "Males are pigs," she said.

Richard looked bewildered.

"I could re-consider," it said doubtfully.

Michael swirled his glass of sherry, then looked at Gloriosa, who sullenly folded her arms across her chest. "I think your decision was correct," Michael said.

"Excellent." It smiled. "I shall be male and I shall adopt a male name. What would you suggest?"

"Something neutral and unobtrusive. How about John?"

"John is *too* neutral," Curly said. "It's so neutral that it sounds suspicious."

Michael smiled. "Pick one," he said. "It's up to you."

"Very well. How about Andrew? Andrew Sloane?"

Rosanna and Curly looked at each other. Rosanna raised an eyebrow.

"Sounds neutral enough to me," Michael said.

"Very well." It gave them a huge smile. "The next time you see me, I shall be a human male named Andrew Sloane." It rubbed its hands together. "I am excited."

Michael, who had seen enough excitement lately, merely shrugged, and so they finished their dinner in peace and drifted off to bed.

Chapter 33

The man standing by the head of the table had introduced himself as Admiral Joshua Haynes. He was tall and probably used to be well built but he had the beginnings of a paunch. The Admiral did not look happy, which Michael thought not at all surprising. "Please sit down," the Admiral said.

Michael had been given a seat in the middle of the table. He was surrounded by an assortment of high ranking officers, eight of whom were male, three female. All of them were frowning, except for Captain Weston, who gave Michael a half-hearted grin.

"First of all," Admiral Haynes said, "I wish to express our most sincere thanks for the information Mr. Glover has brought us." Most of the assembled officers looked more rebellious than thankful. The Admiral glowered around the table.

"Why is this man here? We've received his report. What else is he supposed to contribute?" The man who was speaking wore an Admiral's stars. He was thin, with close cut brown hair, hollow cheeks and a strong jaw. His name tag said, *Flynn, Eamon.*

Privately, Michael wondered the same thing.

Admiral Haynes scowled. "Mr. Glover has given us invaluable information on the events in the Rift. Without him, we would have no idea what happened to our fleet. He is a registered civilian associate with the Imperial Navy and has made initial contact with two previously unknown systems."

"Anybody with a ship can make contact with previously unknown systems," Reynolds said. "They're everywhere."

"In addition," said Haynes, "Mr. Glover's starship appears to be more advanced than any currently in our possession."

Flynn huffed out a breath and sank back into his seat.

"Now," Haynes said, "for the benefit of our guest, let's go around the table and introduce ourselves."

They did so without further argument, giving their names and rank.

A woman, tall, red-headed and muscular, wearing Captain's bars, leaned forward. Her name was Theresa Adams. "Tell me, Mr. Glover, where did you obtain your ship?"

Michael had been expecting that question. "It's an old First Empire design," he said. "I came across it on an abandoned world." It was the truth, sort of.

A Captain at the other end of the table, who had been listening with a mulish expression on his face, said, "I think we should commandeer it. This is an emergency situation. We need all the advantages we can get."

They would find commandeering the *London* to be more difficult than they expected. Michael hoped it didn't come to that.

Admiral Haynes frowned and actually looked for a moment to be considering the idea, then he shook his head. "No," he said. "Mr. Glover had no need to come forward. The fact that he has done so is laudable. We will not re-pay his patriotism, and his generosity, by stealing his ship."

Wise, Michael thought. There were at least a thousand as yet undiscovered worlds out there that the First Empire once occupied. As Admiral Flynn had said, the Second Empire made contact with previously unknown systems every year. Most had fallen into barbarism and decay but many offered advanced and substantial technology. It was official Empire policy to treat all new worlds and people with respect, to open diplomatic relations where possible and to leave their property alone.

"Any other objections?" Admiral Haynes looked around the table. No one spoke. "Very well, let's get to it." A hologram appeared in the tank over the middle of the table. "This is a graph of pirate activity in this sector. As you can see, there has been a steady increase over the past five years. I assume that all of you are acquainted with this information?"

The Admiral scanned the table, waiting for any of them to speak. When none did, he went on. "Helios is on the frontier. From High Command's point of view, what happens here is of minimal interest. It does matter to us, however." He smiled thinly. "Since it is our world that was attacked and our fleet that has been destroyed." He looked around the table at his subordinates, most of whom shifted uncomfortably and refused to meet his eyes. "I trust that there is no disagreement on this basic fact? Our jobs, and perhaps our very lives may depend upon the actions that we take in the immediate future. Half of our ships are now gone and the capabilities of the enemy are still unknown.

"So, aside from stealing civilians' ships, what are your suggestions?"

"Strengthen our defenses," Admiral Flynn said.

Haynes nodded. "It's being done."

"We need information," the red-headed captain said.

"Yes, we do. Any ideas on how to get some?"

None of them spoke. A few frowned. A few others appeared thoughtful. Admiral Haynes grinned; not the happiest grin, Michael noted. "Think about it," he said. "I'll expect a summary from each of you by 08:00 tomorrow morning."

The meeting broke up a few minutes later and Michael went back to the hotel. He was only mildly surprised to receive an invitation to meet with Admiral Haynes in his private office at 09:00 the next morning.

That evening, after dinner, he knocked on Andrew Sloane's door. Andrew opened it. By now, he was a tall, fit looking young man, with auburn hair and green eyes. Michael wondered if the changes extended to Andrew's formerly non-existent genitalia, but it seemed impolite to ask. Andrew smiled at him. "Please come in."

Michael entered and sat at the desk. Andrew stood in the center of the little room, smiling down at him.

"Tell me about your people," Michael said, "and then tell me what has been going on in the Rift."

Andrew Sloane blinked and closed his eyes tightly. Something seemed to be bothering him. "Carbon based life forms first came here many millions of years ago," Andrew Sloane said. "They came; they investigated, but they caused no damage to ourselves or to our environment. My people avoided them and they soon left. It was a harsh and inhospitable place for their fragile little bodies and they must have seen no reason to stay.

"Human beings arrived only recently and constructed their base on Helios. These actions were considered benign, or at least neutral. We did not object to them.

163

"Then more humans came. They seemed unaware of us and again, we avoided their notice. They built an installation upon a planetoid near the edges of the torus. Their motivations at first seemed obscure."

"You say they were human? All of them?"

"Yes, entirely human."

Michael nodded. "Good." The fact that the enemy were human was at least minimally reassuring. Better to deal with humans, whose abilities and resources were not likely to be greater than those of the Empire, and whose actions and motivations could at least be understood.

"You should realize," Andrew Sloane said, "that we are placid beings. Though the Rift is deadly to carbon based life forms, to us it is a pleasant, nurturing environment. We evolved slowly, from what beginnings, we do not know. My people have been self-aware for over a billion years. We have never had a major conflict. There was no need. The abundant energy of the Rift supplied all our needs. The company of our fellows uplifted and entertained us. Only at the end of adolescence do my people feel a need to assert themselves, when the urge to reproduce comes upon us, but there are always fellow beings who are willing to meld, and in that melding, new beings are formed, grow within us and bud off. These are soon independent and go their way.

"We do not understand humanity and the other races that, to us, resemble them so closely. The lives that you live are so short, so filled with urgent desires and drama and conflict. We observed the inhabitants of the base near the torus. We found that we disapproved of their actions, but as I said, we are placid beings. A consensus was building to eject them from our domain but it had not yet been reached. Instead, it was decided to create me." Andrew Sloane smiled and gestured down at himself. "This body that you see before you."

"I have acquainted myself with your science, your philosophy and theology, your art and your legends. Like the Christ child and his heavenly father, my father and I are one, and one day, we shall be re-united, but until that day, I am to sojourn in the human worlds. I am to observe. I am to gather the data that we require to determine our future attitude toward humanity and its associated races. I am to participate, as much as I am able, in the life of mankind. For a little while, I shall be one of you." He smiled, and swayed a bit to one side.

Michael blinked. "That's very nice, Andrew. Your resemblance to the Christ child is certainly marvelous." Michael had knocked on Andrew's door hoping to get some information regarding pirate activity and had been immediately subjected to Andrew's rather long and portentous declaration. Now that he looked closer, Andrew appeared a bit glassy eyed. "Have you been drinking?" Michael asked.

"Yes," Andrew said. He gave Michael a wide, beatific smile.

"Oh." Andrew was swaying, first to one side, then the other. He seemed to be unaware of this fact. "Perhaps you should sit down," Michael said.

Andrew drew himself up. "No need. My body will metabolize the alcohol within a few minutes. I drank a bottle of your brandy. I wished to experience the effects." He frowned. "I am still uncertain why you do this. From my reading, I gather that this particular effect is called 'nausea'."

"Probably." Michael clucked his tongue. "You're lucky. Most people who drink an entire bottle of brandy are nauseous for quite awhile." He frowned. "Are you going to throw up?"

Andrew considered this question for a long moment. Then he cleared his throat. "I do not believe so."

Andrew knew everything that his people knew or surmised regarding human action in the Rift. Pirate activity had begun over twenty years before and slowly increased. It was not possible to follow a vessel through the warped reality of slipspace but an emerging ship always retained its original vector. The ships had come from three different directions, one from the adjoining sector, one from outside human occupied space and one from the heart of the Empire. The installation in the torus had served as a meeting place, trading center and re-fueling station. What went on inside was not known to the people of the Rift but they could make assumptions. Bodies would occasionally be ejected onto the asteroid's surface. These bodies were almost always young, sometimes female but most often male. They had died violently.

Often, their limbs were shackled together. There were marks of what appeared to be torture on their flesh.

"We are still ignorant of your customs," Andrew said, "but my people would not treat other sentient beings in such a fashion." He frowned. "This behavior offended us. It seemed unethical." By now, the effects of the alcohol had entirely worn off. Andrew appeared quite sober.

"Yes," Michael said. "I should think so."

Andrew shook his head sadly. "You have supplied me with access to everything that is known regarding human history and the thoughts of your greatest minds, including their ideas regarding ethics and moral philosophy. It is a fact that many of your cultures regarded those outside their tribe or peer grouping to be less than human, and therefore not subject to the usual protections of custom and law. Often the customs—and sometimes the law—explicitly denied outsiders any protection at all. They could be eliminated, merely for convenience; they could be enslaved, kept as property and used in any fashion that their owners preferred."

"I was a soldier," Michael said, "not a philosopher. Perhaps I'm not the best one to have this conversation with. We like to think that we are more enlightened than our ancestors but some of our thinkers maintain that there are no absolute rules of morality or behavior," Michael shrugged. "History records numerous events of which we are not proud but today, those who abuse other intelligent beings are thought by the large majority of mankind to be criminals, and even the criminals most often share this judgment of themselves. Criminals rarely try to justify their actions. They know that what they are doing is wrong. Most of them just don't care."

Andrew frowned. "Does this make them evil? Or does it make them sociopaths?"

In his prior life, and particularly in the midst of strangling the life out of an enemy, Michael had often asked himself the same question. "I'm not sure there's a difference."

"Ah, but one is a choice; the other is a condition beyond the individual's control. Is a lion or a tiger evil if it kills and eats a man? Or is it merely following its nature?"

"A lion or a tiger has limited ability to reason," Michael said. "Notions of right and wrong are meaningless to it."

"But are such notions meaningless to a sociopath?"

"The sociopath lacks a conscience but he does not lack a mind. He knows what the rules are. He chooses to either obey them, or not."

"But this is mere expedience," Andrew declared, "not conviction. The sociopath, if he does indeed choose to follow the rules of your society, does so out of a desire to avoid punishment, not because he believes that he should."

Michael shrugged. "He believes that he should avoid punishment. The end result is the same, or it ought to be."

Andrew frowned. He was silent. Finally, he looked up at Michael and said, "I am not convinced."

Michael sighed. "Well, you'll have a long time to think about it." He rose to his feet. "And on that note," he said, "I am going to bed."

"This was transmitted only recently. None of my people have seen it yet." Haynes leaned over the desk and handed Michael a sheet of paper. It contained a graph, similar to the one shown at yesterday's meeting. "Pirate activity in the sectors surrounding our own," Haynes said.

The graph showed a slow but steady increase over at least ten years. The Admiral gave him a mirthless smile. "It involves a significant portion of the Empire's periphery, and there have even been some isolated attacks near the core worlds.

"High Command is"—the Admiral grimaced—"worried."

No kidding, Michael thought. "I can understand that," he said. "Why are you telling me?"

Haynes sat back in his seat and smiled without humor. "We call them pirates but that may be a misnomer. Perhaps invaders would be a better term. Or possibly insurgents."

Adversaries often attempted to destabilize their opposition prior to invasion. Invaders and insurgents often went hand in hand. Michael nodded. "Go on," he said.

"You don't seem surprised."

"I'm not."

The Admiral frowned. "It's impossible to believe that these incidents are isolated. There does not appear to be any obvious coordination between them but nobody in a position to know what is going on believes that."

"A conspiracy," Michael said. "A very large conspiracy."

"So it would appear."

The Second Empire was determined not to repeat the mistakes of the past. The First Empire had ruthlessly enforced its hegemony. Better to be feared than loved. The First Empire had tolerated little dissent and zero disobedience, and the system had worked for over four thousand years. The Second Empire preferred to be loved, or at least respected. The Second Empire, built upon the remnants of the old, was a cobbled together affair, more of a commonwealth than a united polity.

Of the more than two thousand worlds that had comprised the First Empire, at least fifty had retained or re-discovered the ability to travel between the stars. At least half of these had either settled new worlds or had co-opted previously settled worlds into their own little empires, confederations or multi-world nations, sometimes by force. Upon being discovered by the Second Empire, most of these had seen the advantages of joining together into a larger political unit, but all had been allowed to retain their own military capability and most had been allowed to retain their own political systems. Some things were not tolerated, of course, like slavery, or forcible annexation of ones' neighbors; Michael had not lied to the Duke of Norlin. And some things were insisted upon, like the freedom to travel and at least some minimal participation by the citizenry in the prevailing government, but in general, most of the member worlds were allowed to do as they pleased.

The Second Empire wanted to give its member states no reason to revolt, but as the Duke of Norlin had said to Michael, sometimes they revolted, anyway. The Second Empire possessed more military might than any of its component parts, but those parts, if banded together, could nevertheless pose a significant threat.

"So," Michael said, "what do you want from me?"

The Admiral smiled thinly. "We want you to be a spy."

Of course you do, Michael thought. He considered the proposal for a long moment, thinking back to that day, so many years in the past, when he had first been offered this very same choice, then he

168

nodded his head slowly and returned the Admiral's smile. "I can do that," he said.

The End

Information about the Chronicles of the Second Interstellar Empire of Mankind

I hope you enjoyed *The Empire of Dust*.

The series continues in *The Empire of Ruin: Book Four of the Chronicles of the Second Interstellar Empire of Mankind*, as Matthew Glover and his crew journey to the heart of the Second Empire and attempt to unravel the conspiracy at the center of the slave trade, a conspiracy which also threatens to engulf the Second Empire in an all-out war for freedom and survival. Please read on for a preview of the *Empire of Ruin*.

For more information, please visit my website, http://www.robertikatz.com or my Facebook page, https://www.facebook.com/Robertikatzofficial/. For continuing updates regarding new releases, author appearances and general information about my books and stories, sign up for my newsletter/email list at http://www.robertikatz.com/join and you will also receive two **free short stories.** The first is a science fiction story, entitled "Adam," about a scientist who uses a tailored retrovirus to implant the Fox P2 gene (sometimes called the language gene) into a cage full of rats and a mouse named Adam, and the unexpected consequences that result. The second is a prequel to the Kurtz and Barent mysteries, entitled "Something in the Blood," featuring Richard Kurtz as a young surgical resident on an elective rotation in the Arkansas mountains, solving a medical mystery that spans two tragic generations.

Preview: The Empire of Ruin: Book Four of the Chronicles of the Second Interstellar Empire of Mankind

Chapter 1

"Canape, sir?"

Michael surveyed the tray of assorted tidbits held out to him by the little drone and selected a mushroom stuffed with crab meat. The crab, nearly four meters long and armed with pincers that could easily decapitate a tiger, had been confined in a holding tank until an hour before the party, when it had been electrocuted and then rendered down into succulent, tender morsels. "Thank you," he said.

"My pleasure, sir," the drone said, and floated on toward the next party-goer.

It's good to be rich, Michael thought. His suit resembled an ancient tuxedo but it was as light as air and fit him like a second skin. Men, women and a scattering of alien beings, some waddling on three legs, a few floating with the aid of anti-gravity belts, a few others skittering across the polished marble floor on stiff, black exoskeletons, all of them dressed in elegant, obviously expensive clothing wandered through the enormous room, mingling, chattering and occasionally idly discussing deals and arrangements that would affect the flow of billions of Empire credits and the lives of thousands of employees.

Michael smiled. *Rich*, he thought again. Pity it wasn't real. Then again, considering the fact that he owned the *London*, the *London*'s cargo and the size of his current credit balance, it pretty much was. Upper middle class, at least, or lower upper, if he wanted to stretch it, and hopefully a lot more to come.

"Mr. Barrad," Johnathon Prescott Jones said, "welcome to Prescott House."

"Thank you, sir. It's a pleasure."

The Prescott Corporation maintained a sizeable corporate retreat on the very little, but very important world of Dancy, with its own private beach, Empire class restaurants and notable spa. A week at Prescott House was a favorite perk of the corporate elite young and old and while in residence, the Prescott Jones family lived in private quarters occupying the top two floors of the main building. The party to which Michael had been invited occupied the main ballroom.

The older Prescott Jones, for many years CEO and Chairman of the Board of the Prescott Corporation, looked nothing like his nephew, so recently deceased in a skiing accident on the winter resort habitat of Kodiak (or so the official story went). He was tall, well-built and tanned, with sharp gray eyes and a ready smile.

"You have an interesting reputation," Prescott Jones said.

Michael smiled, sipped his drink and modestly said nothing. Prescott Jones smiled back. "The example that you represent is enticing. I wish that I had the freedom to travel the space-ways, but I'm afraid that corporations do not run themselves."

Michael gave a negligent shrug and signaled to a drone carrying a tray full of champagne. The drone drifted toward them. Michael deposited his empty glass on the tray, selected a new one and sipped, nodding his head. The champagne was excellent. "This is true," he said, "but they don't have to be run by you or by me. You could delegate all of it and spend your life doing whatever amuses you."

Prescott Jones looked for a moment as if he was considering this idea, then he smiled wistfully. "The Prescott Corporation is successful and growing. I flatter myself that it would not be so successful if someone with a less immediate interest were in charge."

Michael raised an eyebrow. "Your nephew did not share your convictions."

Prescott Jones blinked. "My nephew," he said.

"Paul Prescott Jones. I met him recently, shortly before his demise, on Kodiak."

Johnathon Prescott Jones stared at him. He wrinkled his nose and glanced away. "My nephew and I disagreed about many things."

"I found him to be a generous and charming man."

"Did you?" Prescott Jones seemed surprised at this. "My nephew had a simple approach to things. He had no need to strive and so he didn't. It does not do to speak ill of the dead, but he lived a frivolous life. I would have been bored."

"Perhaps he had other interests of which you were unaware." No *perhaps* about it; but Johnathan Prescott Jones' apparently was indeed unaware of his late nephew's criminal inclinations. His heartbeat did not increase. The scent of fear, or even of interest, was not present.

Prescott Jones stared at him. "I doubt that," he said.

Michael shrugged. "He fancied himself a gourmet and was very proud of his chef. I attended a number of dinner parties at his residence." Michael allowed his eyes to sweep around the capacious room. "A small estate. Nothing so grand as this."

Prescott Jones nodded his head. "Well, I'm glad you're enjoying yourself," he said, then he seemed to spot something in the crowd. "Excuse me. There is somebody I need to speak with."

"Of course," Michael said. "Thank you again for inviting me."

"Space is wide," General Haynes had said. "There are hundreds of settled worlds and many of these worlds keep records poorly, or not at all. There are billions of people who don't officially exist on any Empire census, and frankly, there are many thousands of others, maybe millions, who are listed incorrectly.

"We take a laissez-faire attitude because we don't have any choice but it's a difficult environment to guarantee security. Anybody can assume a false identity. Anybody might be something other than what he seems." The General sat back in his seat, frowning.

Tell me about it, Michael thought. He held his hands beneath his chin and tapped his fingers together. "There are advantages, as well. I would think that the situation can be made to work in your favor."

The General blinked and gave him a long, slow smile. "Somehow, I imagine that you know all this?" It wasn't really a question.

Michael shrugged.

He had been offered the rank of Commander in the Imperial Navy and placed on indefinite assignment. Michael had been reluctant at first to accept the arrangement but General Haynes had reassured him. "You won't be hobbled by it. We know that you're not really a military man." The General's eyes flickered at this statement, and he almost smiled. Michael said nothing. "I understand your reluctance to place yourself under someone else's command. You can resign the commission at any time. You'll be an independent agent. The rank is for your own benefit, in case you need to prove your *bona fides*, or to call on us for assistance."

"Put it in writing," Michael said.

"Naturally," the General replied stiffly, and on that basis, Michael had accepted. There were advantages to the situation. The *London* would be listed as a civilian vessel under military contract and he would no longer need to purchase supplies. Any Naval installation would give him what he requested, no questions asked. They provided him with a series of pre-programmed identities, for himself and all his crew; and they gave him some additional personnel, a squadron of Imperial Marines, plus a "liaison" named Henrik Anson, officially in charge of the marine contingent but whose real function, Michael suspected, was to keep an eye on Michael. That was fine with Michael, since the arrangement allowed him to keep an eye on Anson, and by extension, on his superiors. It was always easier to spy on a spy, Michael reflected, if you knew who he was and where he happened to be.

For now, Michael was Luciano Barrad, the heir to an asteroid mining facility that had, many centuries ago, branched out into volatile hydrocarbons extracted from the cores of gas-giants. The asteroid had long since been mined out, the need for energy derived from hydrocarbons vanished with the re-discovery of reliable fusion and EM technology. No matter; the money had been safely invested and Barrad Holdings now owned shares in nearly a thousand different corporations. Luciano Barrad was very rich indeed. He commanded his own ship. He went where he wished and did as he pleased.

There had been five different Luciano Barrads before Michael Glover. It was one of the more popular identities maintained by military intelligence.

Dancy was a small world of placid, blue skies, warm seas and tropical lagoons, only twenty light-years from Reliance, the capital world of the Empire. Terra Nova was the only large city on Dancy. Almost all of the largest corporations, richest men and women and most important families maintained a residence on Dancy. It was customary for the government to adjourn to the little world during the annual three month Winter recess, when Reliance wandered far from its sun and the capital world grew cold, rainy and dark.

Follow the money, always a good idea when conducting an investigation, and no world possessed more money than Dancy.

The slave trade was spreading outward from the edges of Imperial space, growing like a cancer. There had been numerous attacks on merchant ships, habitats and even naval installations. Somebody had to be making money by buying and selling slaves, or at least obtaining some advantage from the disruption, or there would be no reason to do it.

"He wasn't sweating," Michael said, "And his heart rate didn't change at all when I mentioned his nephew."

Henrik Anson was tall, fit and lean, with a thin scar across one cheek. He looked at Michael moodily. "You can tell that?" he asked.

"Yes."

Anson pursed his lips. "A useful talent," he said.

Anson's rank was Colonel. He was the commanding officer of the small marine contingent aboard the *London*. Though his official rank was higher than Michael's, the *London* was Michael's ship and his contract with the military left no doubt that Michael, not Anson, was in charge.

In actuality, while Anson and his ten marines had presumably started their careers in the more traditional branches of the Service, all of them, Michael was fairly certain, were trained as spies. Michael was not certain if Anson knew that Michael knew this, but since neither of them were fools, it had to be assumed. It also had to be assumed that the main object of Anson's spying was Michael and the other members of his unconventional crew, possibly with a goal of taking over the ship if opportunity presented. Anson was given a room of his own in the same corridor as Curly, Andrew Sloane and the others. His men were housed in comfortable but somewhat less luxurious quarters one deck below, alongside his contingent of twenty Illyrian mercenaries.

Michael had appointed Anson his Chief of Security, not that he needed one. Anson, to Michael's complete lack of surprise, filled the role excellently.

So now, Anson knew that Michael's senses were enhanced. It might have been smarter to keep this information to himself but after giving the question careful thought, Michael had decided that a bit of intimidation might just make Anson hesitate to push things. Romulus, for the duration of this mission, was confining himself inside his wall panel. Anson had no idea of Romulus' existence and many of the London's other capabilities, and Michael's as well, were not apparent, either to the Marines or the Illyrians bunking on the lower deck.

"So, he's not lying," Anson said.

"Or he's very good at controlling his reactions. Outwardly, he clearly disapproved of his nephew's dissolute lifestyle."

Anson's lips twitched. "But does he know more about his nephew's activities than he admits? And what exactly was Paul Prescott Jones doing on Kodiak, anyway?"

"Paul Prescott Jones is dead. He's no longer in a position to commit mischief; and he was nowhere near the center of the conspiracy, whatever it really is. Paul Prescott Jones was middle management. He identified ships that could be easily taken, passenger ships with little or no defensive capability, along with their itineraries, and he received a share of the profits. Exactly where he placed in their hierarchy is a question mark. Judging by the fact that he wasn't invited along when Cabot, Crane and Rivas made their escape, I think we can assume that he was not regarded as a significant player."

"So who would a billionaire playboy, who didn't need the money and was presumably just doing it for kicks, choose to work for?"

"We have no evidence that it was his uncle," Michael said.

Anson frowned. "No. Not yet."

The stands surrounding the race track were filled. The sky overhead was blue and almost cloudless, the day pleasantly cool.

Michael Glover sat in an elevated box, waiting while the sand was raked and the worst of the spilled blood removed. "I thought these things were fed before the race?" he said.

The groom frowned. "Some trainers believe that they run better if they're hungry."

Michael grunted. The last race had turned into chaos when one of the giant, mutated cheetahs had turned on its rider. Incited by the smell of blood, the other animals had joined in the feast. The hapless rider's screams were abruptly cut off when one of the cheetahs crushed his skull and swallowed his brain. By the time the guards arrived with tranquilizer guns and shock prods, the rider had been reduced to a few scattered shreds of flesh. "That seems unwise," Michael said.

The groom swallowed and diplomatically said nothing.

"Luciano." Michael looked up. The man standing at the rail to his box was of indeterminate age, like most of the adults on this world. He was tall and thin, with sharp green eyes and a strong chin. He wore simple summer clothing that was well made but not ostentatious. His name was David Armstrong, a co-owner of Bratton Associates, a corporation that manufactured antique watercraft and modern spacing yachts. Michael had met him at a party a week before and found him to be a keen observer of Dancy's social scene.

"David, please sit down."

David smiled and slid into an empty seat, then poured himself a glass of spiced wine from the pitcher sitting on a low table. "Cheers," he said.

Wordlessly, Michael held out his own glass for a re-fill. "I was thinking of buying a racing cheetah," he said, "but I'm starting to have second thoughts."

"I would advise against it," David said. "It's an expensive occupation and very few are successful at it. Those who are, know what they're doing."

Michael shrugged. "You're probably right. Perhaps not a hobby for a dilettante."

By now, the sand had been raked smooth and the next race was about to start. "I've put a hundred credits on Red Fang," David said.

The starting gate snapped open and seven big cats raced out, their riders clinging to the reins. David leaned forward and stared at the track, lips parted, his breath coming faster. The cheetahs covered ground at an amazing pace, their legs moving like pistons. The race was over in less than a minute. Red Fang came in third.

David sat back in his seat. "Damn," he said.

Bull by the horns, Michael thought. "Tell me," he said, "what do you think of Johnathon Prescott Jones?"

"Pleasant enough fellow," David said. "He throws a nice party. He's been good for the company. They were adrift for too long."

"So I've heard." Michael sipped his drink. "I met his nephew recently, before his unfortunate demise."

David frowned and glanced at him sideways. "Did you?" His voice seemed a trifle guarded, Michael thought.

"Have you ever been to Kodiak?"

"I don't believe I've ever heard of it."

"A winter habitat. Paul Prescott Jones maintained a residence there."

David frowned. "To each his own. I never liked winter."

"Apparently, neither did Prescott Jones. His residence included a tropical oasis under a dome."

"He could have kept the tropics without the dome if he had stayed here."

"True, but sometimes the urge to get away from the demands of one's family is overwhelming." Michael smiled. "Tell me, who were his friends?"

"Why do you ask?" David gave him a curious look.

"He seemed like a rather introverted fellow. He gave a dinner party now and then and he had a mistress or two but he kept to himself, mostly. I wondered."

"I didn't know him all that well. From what I recall, he was close to his sister, and he spent a lot of time with George Seferis and..."—a faraway look crept over David's face—"what was his name? Oh, yes: Peter Westing, and also Raleigh Gaines." David frowned. "None of them have done much with their lives, but then, they're rich, so they don't need to."

"No," Michael said with a satisfied smile. "I suppose not."

Printed in Great Britain
by Amazon

31219904R00101